· IRISH MYTH AND LEGEND ·

Salerni

The Names Upon the Harp

BY **MARIE HEANEY** ILLUSTRATED BY **P. J. LYNCH**

SCHOLASTIC INC.

New York Toronto London Auckland Sydney
Mexico City New Delhi Hong Kong Buenos Aires

THIS BOOK IS DEDICATED TO THE MEMORY OF
MY PARENTS AND TO MY SISTERS AND BROTHER
WHO LIVED WITH ME IN TIR NA N-OG
—M. H. ·

FOR NEASA
—P. J. L.

Arthur A. Levine Books hardcover edition designed by Kristina Albertson, published by Arthur A. Levine Books, an imprint of Scholastic Press, November 2000

ISBN 0-590-68060-9

12 11 10 9 8 7 6 5 4 3 2 1   1 2 3 4 5
6/0

Printed in the U.S.A.   14

First Scholastic paperback printing, September 2001

The art for this book was created with watercolors and gouache on Arches paper. The text was set in 12-point Aries, a typeface designed by Eric Gill in 1932.
Calligraphy by Bernard Maisner

TABLE OF CONTENTS

PART ONE: THE MYTHOLOGICAL CYCLE

Moytura   *8*

The Children of Lir   *20*

PART TWO: THE ULSTER CYCLE

The Birth of Cuchulainn   *30*

Bricriu's Feast   *38*

Deirdre of the Sorrows   *50*

PART THREE: THE FINN CYCLE

Finn & the Salmon of Knowledge   *62*

"Summer" *Translated from the Irish by Seamus Heaney*   *71*

The Enchanted Deer   *72*

Oisin in the Land of Youth   *80*

PRONUNCIATION GUIDE   *92*

SOURCE NOTES   *94*

FURTHER READING   *95*

AUTHOR'S NOTE

*"... you and I leave
names upon the harp"*
CUCHULAINN TO CONOR,
FROM *ON BAILE'S STRAND*
BY W. B. YEATS

THE STORIES IN THIS BOOK have been known to the Irish for centuries. They are preserved in manuscripts hundreds of years old, but long before they were written down by scribes in early Irish monasteries, they had been told at feasts and gatherings by storytellers and bards, and were still told until recently.

Scholars have divided early Irish literature into three main cycles: the Mythological cycle, the Ulster cycle, and the Fenian cycle. In this book, I have given a brief introduction to each of these cycles and included tales from each. But I have chosen the stories not merely because they are old or representative, but because they have entertained and moved listeners and readers for generations, and still have the power to do so.

THE MYTHOLOGICAL CYCLE

The Tuatha De Danaan, the People of the Goddess Danu, were a divine race who possessed great magical powers and were learned and gifted, according to Irish legend. They came to Ireland to take over the country, and when they landed, they set fire to their boats so there would be no turning back. The smoke from the burning boats darkened the sun and filled the land for three days, and the Fir Bolgs, who lived there, thought the Tuatha De Danaan had arrived in a magic mist.

The Tuatha De Danaan defeated the Fir Bolgs and became rulers of Ireland, but another enemy, the demonic Fomorians, enslaved and tyrannized them until they too were defeated at the battle of Moytura.

After this victory, the Tuatha De Danaan ruled Ireland for many years, until they were defeated by another wave of invaders, the Milesians. Although they were banished by these newcomers, they did not leave Ireland. Instead, they went underground to live in the *sidhes*, mounds and earthworks that are scattered all over the country.

Above them, the human inhabitants of Ireland, descendants of the Milesians, lived and died, and were helped but sometimes hindered by the Tuatha De Danaan, who became known as the People of the Sidhe, the Faery, or the Little Folk. From time to time, these mysterious beings would enter the mortal world, on Halloween and May Day in particular, to mingle with humans and come and go in their affairs. But they always returned to their kingdom under the earth, that happy otherworld, the Land of Youth.

MOYTURA

ONG, LONG AGO IN IRELAND A GREAT BATTLE FOR MASTERY OF the island took place at Moytura. The struggle was between two powerful tribes: the Tuatha De Danaan and the Fomorians.

The Tuatha De Danaan were a divine people whose king, Nuada, ruled the country wisely and justly. At his court at Tara were feastings and entertainments of all kinds, and everyone had plenty to eat and drink.

Their enemies, the demonic Fomorians, were fierce sea-pirates who lived on the islands scattered round the western coast. Their leader was known as Balor of the Evil Eye and he was feared for his cruelty. It was through a magic spell that Balor had got his power and his name. One day when he was a boy he heard chanting inside the house where the magicians gathered to work new spells. Seeing a window open high in the wall, he scrambled up and looked furtively through it, but the room was so full of fumes and gases that he could see nothing. As he peered through the window the chants grew louder, and a strong plume of smoke rose in the air straight into Balor's face. Instantly he was blinded and could not open one of his eyes. He struggled to the ground, writhing with pain, and at that moment one of the magicians came out of the house. "That spell we were making was a spell of death," he said to Balor, "and the fumes from it have brought the power of death to your eye."

Among his own people Balor's eye remained shut, but when he opened it against his enemies, they dropped dead at his fearsome stare. As he grew older his eyelid grew heavier until, in the end, he could not open it without help. An ivory ring was driven though the lid and through this ring ropes were threaded to make a pulley. It took ten men to raise the great, heavy lid, but

8

ten times that number were slain at a single glance. His evil eye made him of great importance to the Fomorians, and he became the most powerful of them all. His ships raided Ireland again and again, and Balor's pirates made slaves of the learned people of the Tuatha De Danaan.

But Balor had a secret fear. One of his druids had foretold that he would die at the hand of his own grandson. Balor had only one child, a daughter called Eithlinn, so he built a tower and shut the girl up in it with twelve women to guard her.

He warned the women that Eithlinn should never see a man, nor hear a man's name mentioned. With Eithlinn imprisoned in the tower Balor felt safe, for without a husband Eithlinn could not have a child and he could not die at his grandson's hand.

Eithlinn grew up into a beautiful woman, well cared for by her companions, but in spite of their kindness she felt lonely. The same man would appear to her again and again in her dreams, and she felt a longing to meet this person. And one day, through Balor's greed, she had her chance.

Balor had plenty of cattle, but he particularly coveted one wonderful cow, which belonged to Cian, a man of the Tuatha De Danaan. This marvelous cow never ran dry, and Balor wanted it so much that he would disguise himself and follow Cian around, waiting for a chance to seize the cow.

One day Balor saw Cian and his brother go to a forge to get some weapons made. Cian went into the forge while his brother stayed outside with the cow. Balor saw his chance. Turning himself into a redheaded boy, he went up to the man who stood with the cow and began to talk to him.

"Are you getting a sword made as well?" he asked.

"I am," said the brother, "in my turn. When Cian comes out of the forge he'll guard the cow and I'll go into the forge and get my weapon made."

"That's what you think!" said the boy. "Your brother has tricked you. He is using all the iron for himself, and there'll be none left for you!"

At this, the man stuffed the cow's halter into the boy's hand and ran into the forge to confront his brother. Instantly Balor threw off his disguise and dragged the cow back to the safety of his own island.

Cian was determined to retrieve his cow, so he went to a woman druid called Birog to ask for help.

Birog disguised Cian as a woman and then conjured up a wind so strong that she and Cian were carried off high in the air.

The wind dropped, and they landed safely on Balor's island at the foot of the tower where Eithlinn was imprisoned. Birog begged Eithlinn's guardians to let them in, saying they were escaping from enemies who wanted to kill them. The women took pity and agreed.

As soon as they were inside, Birog cast another spell and all the women, except Eithlinn, fell fast asleep. Cian, who had cast off his woman's clothes, ran up the stairs to the top of the tower. There, all alone, he found the most beautiful woman he had ever seen, gazing sadly out to sea. As he stared at her, Eithlinn turned round and recognized Cian as the one she had dreamt about so often. They were both overjoyed and, declaring their love for each other, they embraced with delight.

When morning came Cian wanted to take Eithlinn from her prison and bring her home with him, but Birog was so terrified of Balor that she swept Cian away from Eithlinn on another enchanted wind and took him back with her to Ireland. Eithlinn was brokenhearted when Cian left her, but she was comforted when she discovered that she would give birth to his child. In due course a boy was born, and she called him Lugh.

When Balor heard the news of his grandson's birth he made up his mind to kill the infant straight away and he gave orders that the baby be thrown into the sea. Wrapped in a blanket held in place by a pin, Lugh was cast into the current by Eithlinn's guardians. As the weeping women watched, the pin opened and the baby rolled into the sea, leaving the empty blanket spread over the waves. Balor felt safe once more. Now he had no grandson to bring about his end.

But Lugh had been saved. Birog, who had been riding the winds, saw what happened and lifted the baby out of the water and carried him safely back

to his father. Cian was overjoyed, and Lugh was fostered out to a king's daughter, who loved him as if he were her own child.

In his foster home Lugh learnt many skills. Craftsmen taught him to work in wood and metal. Champions and athletes trained him to perform amazing feats. From poets and musicians he heard the stories of the heroes and learnt to play on the harp and timpan. The court physician taught him the use of herbs and elixirs to cure illness, and the magicians revealed to him their secret powers. He grew up as skillful as he was handsome, and when he had learnt every skill that his fosterer could teach him, Lugh made up his mind to go join the king's household. He gathered a group of warriors around him and set off for Tara. As he rode up to the gates of Nuada's Fort Camall, the doorkeeper challenged him.

"Who are you," he asked, "and why have you come here?"

"I am Lugh of the Long Arm," the warrior said, "son of Cian and Eithlinn, and grandson of Balor. Tell the king I want to join his household!"

"No one finds a place in Nuada's household unless he has a special art," said Camall, "so I must ask you what art you have."

"I am master of all the arts," said Lugh. "Go and ask the king if he has in the household any single person who has all the skills. If he has, I will leave these gates and will no longer try to enter Tara."

Camall ran off to take Lugh's message to the king. "Let us see if he is as talented as he claims!" Nuada said. "Bring the chess board out to him and let him compete against our best players."

Lugh played against the best chess players in the land and won every game until there was no one left unbeaten.

Then Nuada said, "Let this young hero in! We have never seen his like before in Tara."

Camall opened the gates, and Lugh entered the fort. He went straight to

the hall where Nuada sat surrounded by the most powerful leaders of the Tuatha De Danaan. Lugh passed by them without a word and sat down on the Seat of Wisdom, next to the king. The champions and poets challenged him to a contest of skills, and one by one he outdid them all. Seeing that he possessed the mastery he claimed, the king decided to enlist his aid against Balor and his followers. While Nuada was telling

Lugh about the Fomorian tyranny, another troop of men arrived, as different from Lugh and his followers as night from day. Nuada and his household rose to their feet as soon as they entered, while Lugh looked on in amazement and vexation.

"Why are you rising to your feet for this miserable, hostile rabble when you didn't stand for me?" he cried.

"We must rise," Nuada replied, "or they will kill us all. These are the Fomorians who have come to harry us again!"

Lugh was so furious when he heard this that he drew his sword, rushed at the Fomorians, and killed all but nine of them.

"You should be killed as well!" he told the cringing survivors. "But I'll spare your lives so that you can return to Balor empty-handed and tell him what happened here!"

The terrified messengers fled from Tara and made for the islands of the Fomorians as quickly as they could. When they arrived at Balor's tower and told him about the fate of their companions, his rage was as great as Lugh's.

"Who is this upstart," Balor roared, "who dares to kill my men and send an insulting message back to me?"

His wife, Ceithlinn of the Crooked Teeth, answered him. "I know well who he is from the description these men give of him, and it is bad news for us. He is our own grandson, the son of our daughter, Eithlinn, and he is known as Lugh of the Long Arm. It has been foretold that he will banish the Fomorians from Ireland for all time, and it will be at his hand that you, Balor, will meet your end!"

Balor listened to her, his rage growing with every word. Then he roared, "I'll go to Ireland myself and meet Lugh in battle, and for all his skills, I will overcome my insolent grandson and cut off his head. Then I'll tie that rebellious island to the stern of my ship and tow it back here, and where Ireland once lay there will be empty ocean!"

He marshaled his fearsome army and set out for Ireland.

Meanwhile, Lugh and Nuada had begun to make plans for battle, too, for they knew what Balor would try. They called together all the people who possessed special skills, and Lugh asked each one what contribution he would make toward the struggle.

The magicians told him they would cause the mountains of Ireland to roll toward the Fomorian army, while sheltering the Tuatha De Danaan. The cupbearers promised to bring a great thirst on the Fomorians and then drain the lakes and rivers of Ireland so there would be no water for them to drink, but there would be plenty of water for Nuada's army even if the battle lasted seven years. The smiths, brass-workers, and carpenters swore they would make the strongest spearshafts, swords, and shields. The physician promised to bathe the wounded in a miraculous well so that they would be cured and ready for battle again, and the poet said he would attack the minds of the Fomorians by composing a satirical poem that would cause them to lose heart. Then the Morrigu, the fierce goddess of battlefields, appeared in the shape of a crow. She promised that she would help the Tuatha De Danaan at the hour of their greatest danger and she foretold a victory for them.

"But you must prepare yourself immediately," she said, "for I have seen the

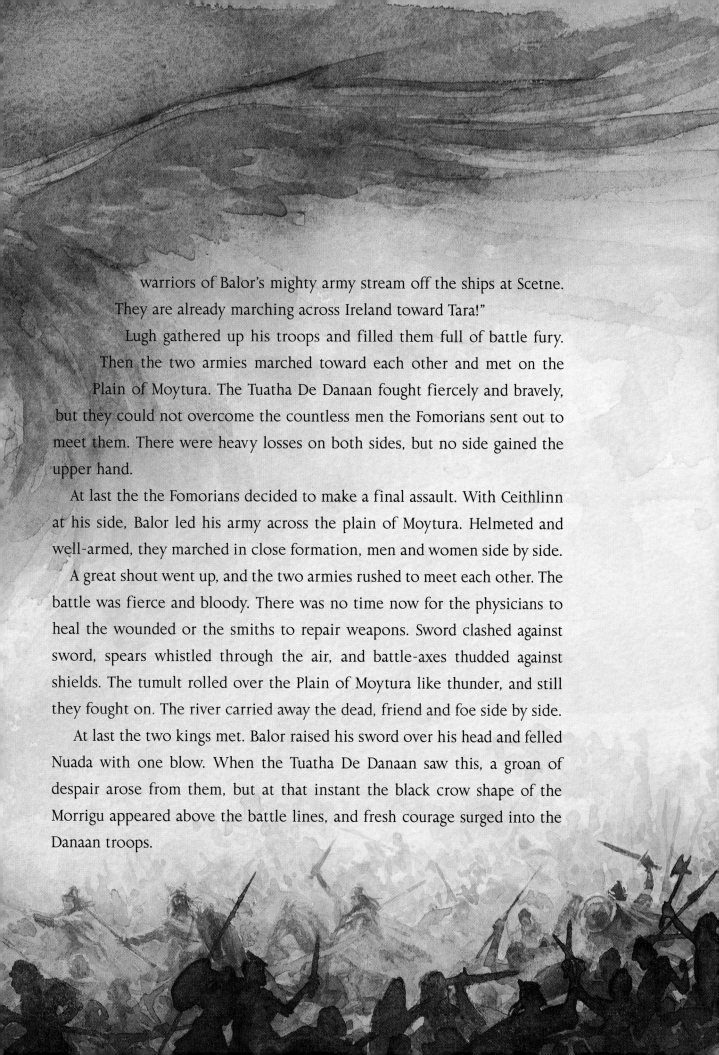

warriors of Balor's mighty army stream off the ships at Scetne. They are already marching across Ireland toward Tara!"

Lugh gathered up his troops and filled them full of battle fury. Then the two armies marched toward each other and met on the Plain of Moytura. The Tuatha De Danaan fought fiercely and bravely, but they could not overcome the countless men the Fomorians sent out to meet them. There were heavy losses on both sides, but no side gained the upper hand.

At last the the Fomorians decided to make a final assault. With Ceithlinn at his side, Balor led his army across the plain of Moytura. Helmeted and well-armed, they marched in close formation, men and women side by side.

A great shout went up, and the two armies rushed to meet each other. The battle was fierce and bloody. There was no time now for the physicians to heal the wounded or the smiths to repair weapons. Sword clashed against sword, spears whistled through the air, and battle-axes thudded against shields. The tumult rolled over the Plain of Moytura like thunder, and still they fought on. The river carried away the dead, friend and foe side by side.

At last the two kings met. Balor raised his sword over his head and felled Nuada with one blow. When the Tuatha De Danaan saw this, a groan of despair arose from them, but at that instant the black crow shape of the Morrigu appeared above the battle lines, and fresh courage surged into the Danaan troops.

Lugh rushed to the side of the dying Nuada and angrily taunted Balor. His abuse drove his grandfather into a rage.

"Lift up my eyelid so I can see the gabbling loudmouth who dares insult me like this!" Balor roared. A terrified hush fell over the multitude as ten Fomorian champions pulled on the ropes to raise the heavy lid. Those nearest to Balor fell down to the earth to escape his deadly stare, but Lugh stood his ground, put a stone in his sling, took aim, and let fly directly at Balor's eye as it opened. The force of the stone drove the eye back through Balor's head, and it landed in the midst of the Fomorian lines. Balor fell dead, and hundreds of his followers were killed by the eye's fatal power.

Then Lugh led a last fierce assault against the Fomorians. With the Morrigu hovering above them, they broke through the enemy lines and drove the Fomorians down to the sea, where they boarded their ships in great haste and set sail for their islands, never to return to Ireland.

THE CHILDREN OF LIR

HERE WAS ONCE A KING IN IRELAND CALLED LIR WHO HAD FOUR children, whom he loved dearly. Fionnuala was his eldest child and she looked after her brothers, Aed, Conn, and Fiacra, because their mother had died when the boys were very young. Lir had his dwelling in the north of the country and he and his children lived happily together there until he brought a new wife, Aoife, home to his fort.

Aoife was jealous of Lir's love for his children. Jealousy turned to hatred, and in the end she could bear the sight of them no longer. One morning she told the children they were going to visit their grandfather, Bodb Dearg, king of the Tuatha De Danaan. The younger children were delighted, but Fionnuala was afraid, for she sensed that Aoife was plotting harm.

Halfway to Bodb's fort they reached Lough Derravaragh and halted. Aoife told the children they could bathe in the lake, and the three boys rushed into the water, splashing and shouting, but Fionnuala hung back. When Aoife saw this she ordered the girl to join her brothers, and Fionnuala waded slowly into the lough.

As soon as the children were all together, Aoife took a druid's wand from the folds of her cloak and, pointing at each child in turn, she chanted a spell: "Children of Lir, your good fortune is over! From now on waterfowl will be your family, and your cries will be mingled with the cries of birds."

In an instant, Fionnuala, Aed, Conn, and Fiacra disappeared, and swimming on the lake were four beautiful white swans.

Aoife turned a deaf ear to their pitiful cries and stared unmoved as the frantic creatures thrashed in the water. Fionnuala rushed to the edge of the lake and stretched her long neck toward her stepmother. "Oh, Aoife!" she begged. "Do not condemn us to be swans forever! If you won't give us back our shape, at least put some limit on this enchantment."

Aoife's icy heart melted as she listened to Fionnuala's desperate pleas. "You will not be swans forever!" she cried. "But you must keep the shape of swans for nine hundred years. You will spend three hundred years here on Lough Derravaragh, three hundred years on the Sea of Moyle, and the last three hundred years by the Atlantic Ocean. When a king from the north marries a queen from the south and you hear the sound of a bell pealing out a new faith, you will know that your exile is over. Till then, though you will have the appearance of swans, you will keep your own minds, your own hearts, and your own voices, and your music will be so sweet that it will console all who hear it. But go away from me now, for the very sight of you torments me!" And horrified by her deed, Aoife ran from the shore to the waiting chariot and galloped to Bodb Dearg's fort.

The king was disappointed to find that the children were not with their stepmother, but Aoife had a story ready. "I came alone," she told Bodb Dearg, "because Lir is jealous of your love for his children and he would not let me bring them to your house!"

At first Bodb Dearg was angry at Aoife's words, but then he became suspicious and he sent a message inviting Lir and his children to visit him the next day. Lir was alarmed. At daybreak he set out for Bodb's fort.

From the middle of Lough Derravaragh the swan-children saw the company approaching and recognized their father at the head. They flew to the lakeside and landed there with a clatter of wings, calling out their father's name. Lir heard his children's voices but he could not see them anywhere. He stood puzzled till suddenly, like a blow to the heart, he understood.

"Fionnuala, Aed, Conn, Fiacra! My beloved children! Oh, how can I help you?" he cried out.

"You cannot help us!" Fionnuala called back. "This is Aoife's work. We are doomed to keep this shape for nine hundred years and no power can change that." Seeing the anguish on Lir's face, she longed to comfort him and she began to sing. Her brothers joined in and, as they sang, Lir's desolation faded. Soothed by the music, he and his household fell into a peaceful sleep.

Next morning Lir set off to tell Bodb Dearg the terrible fate of his children. When the king learned of Aoife's treachery, he turned to her in a fury and with his druid's wand he transformed her into a demon of the air. A bitter blast swept her aloft like a withered leaf, and people say that on a stormy night you can still hear Aoife moaning in the wind.

The next day Lir and Bodb Dearg went to Lough Derravaragh, and there they stayed while years became decades, and decades, centuries. Then one day Fionnuala knew it was time for them to leave. As night fell the swans sang Lir and their friends to sleep for the very last time. At daybreak the four swan-children rose into the air, circled the sorrowful crowd below, and set off for the cold Sea of Moyle.

This sea was a stormy band of water between Ireland and Scotland, lashed by gales in spring, by ice and hail in winter. In this desolate place the children suffered such cold that their feathers became brittle as glass, and every spring they were flung from rock to rock by the gales.

One night a fierce storm rose up. Great black thunderclouds piled up and lightning split the sky, and all night long the swans were scattered in the sea spray. When dawn broke, Fionnuala could hardly fly, but she made her way to the Seal's Rock, Carraignarone, and landed. The sun climbed into a clear sky, but Fionnuala could not see her brothers anywhere.

Suddenly Conn appeared, barely clearing the waves. He landed beside Fionnuala, and she put him under her right wing. A while later Fiacra struggled to the rock, and Fionnuala put him under her left wing. At last Aed arrived, beaten and spent, and crept beneath the feathers of Fionnuala's breast. There they rested till their strength returned.

Three hundred years in that stormy sea passed slowly but at last it was time for the swan-children to go.

"And on the way," Fionnuala told her brothers, "we will fly over our home and see our father." They flew over the lovely landscape of their childhood scanning the ground anxiously for Lir's fort. At last they saw the familiar hill, but there was no sign of their father's house. All that remained was a grassy mound, covered with rocks and weeds. The children of Lir landed among the broken earthworks and, as they cowered there, their feathers ruffled by the winds, they remembered their home as they had left it with Aoife on that fateful morning and their hearts nearly cracked with grief. Keening a lament, they rose into the air and headed west to spend the last three hundred years of their exile.

In a quiet inlet on the western coast of Ireland was a small island called Inish Glora, where the swans would shelter. There they sang, and birds flocked from the other western islands to listen to the matchless music.

A new age had dawned in Ireland and the Tuatha De Danaan had been replaced by another race. The old gods had gone underground, and the people now worshiped the Christian god. The children of Lir, themselves, had become legends.

A hermit called Mochaomhog knew the legend. He sensed that the time of the swan-children's release must be close at hand, so he came to Inish Glora and built a church on the island. Every morning as he began to pray, he rang a bronze bell. One calm morning the sound of the bell pealed out across the lake and woke the children of Lir. Fionnuala was overjoyed, for she knew that the bell announced their freedom, and she began to sing.

Hearing her song, the hermit hurried down toward the lake and in the pale morning light he saw the four swans. He called to them across the water: "Children of Lir, don't be afraid! It is for your sake I have come to this island. Come with me and I will help you!"

The children of Lir trusted the hermit and went ashore. Mochaomhog put a silver chain around their necks so that they would never be parted again, and they lived in his hut, happy and peaceful at last.

While the swan-children were living with the hermit, Lairgren, a king from the north, married a queen from the south, and through this marriage the last part of Aoife's spell was broken. The new queen asked for the swans as a marriage gift, so the king traveled to Inish Glora to get them for her. When Mochaomhog refused his request, the angry king seized the chain that linked the swans and dragged the terrified creatures from the hut. They struggled frantically for a moment, then suddenly the tumult stopped. As Lairgren and Mochaomhog watched in horror, the plumage of the swans fell away, and lying on the the ground were four frail old people. Mochaomhog rushed to their side and tried to comfort them. But Fionnuala said to him, "We are dying, my kind friend. Bury us here where we found peace."

Soon after, the children of Lir died peacefully, and Mochaomhog buried them as Fionnuala had requested and raised a stone over their grave.

THE ULSTER CYCLE

onor Mac Nessa was the king of Ulster and he and his followers, the Red Branch Warriors, lived in a large fort at Armagh, in the north of Ireland. Fergus, Conall, and Laoghaire were among the most famous of Conor's champions, but the greatest of them all was Cuchulainn. The druids, judges, and bards of the Ulster court foretold the future and counseled and entertained the king. The women of Ulster, Emer, Deirdre and Levercham, were strong and forceful.

Conor's fort was called Emain Macha. It was given its name by the goddess Macha after a race in which she had been forced to run against Conor's horses although she was pregnant. When her twins were born, Macha gave a loud scream and the strength of all the men who heard it ebbed away. As she died, Macha cursed the Ulstermen, "From this day forward, you will be afflicted by this weakness because of your cruel treatment of me. At the hour of your greatest need, you will become as powerless as I am now and your descendants will be afflicted in the same way for nine generations. My name is Macha and my name and the name of my twins will stick to this place forever."

These prophecies came true. The fort was called Emain Macha, the Twins of Macha. From then on, and for many years, the Ulstermen lay powerless at the time of their greatest need. Cuchulainn was the only man to escape the weakness, and that was because his father, Lugh, like Macha herself, was one of the Tuatha De Danaan. Here are three of my favorite stories from this cycle.

THE BIRTH OF CUCHULAINN

ENTURIES AGO WHEN CONOR MAC NESSA WAS THE KING OF Ulster, a very strange thing happened at his stronghold at Emain Macha. His sister, Dechtire, and her fifty young companions vanished from the fort without a trace. Neither the king nor any members of his household saw them go, and no one knew anything at all about their whereabouts.

Then one day, three years later, a large flock of birds flew across the country and landed at Emain Macha. As Conor and the Red Branch champions watched aghast, the birds ate everything that grew around the fort.

The king could watch the devastation no longer, so he mounted his horse and he and his companions galloped toward the flock. The birds rose into the air, joined together in pairs by silver chains, and flew south across Slieve Fuad, with the king's party following fast behind.

As daylight began to fade, two birds broke away from the flock and headed toward the cluster of Tuatha De Danaan dwellings on the banks of the Boyne River. The king's company followed, but just as they reached the riverbank a heavy shower of snow fell and they lost sight of the birds. Conor ordered his men to find shelter for the night. Bricriu, the poet, set out on this errand, and as he wandered around in the dark, he heard a strange, low noise. He walked in the direction of the sound, and suddenly, out of nowhere, appeared a large, spacious, well-lit house. Bricriu went to the door and looked in. There before him was a handsome couple, a young warrior richly dressed, and at his side, a beautiful woman.

"You are welcome, Bricriu," said the man. When Bricriu heard the warrior call him by name and saw the beauty and splendor of the young man, he knew he was in the presence of Lugh of the Long Arm, one of the most important personages from the land of the Ever Young.

"You are welcome a thousand times over," said the woman at Lugh's side, smiling with delight.

"Why does your wife greet me so warmly?" Bricriu asked.

"It is on her account that I have welcomed you," Lugh replied. "The woman at my side is Dechtire. It was she and her companions who took on the shape of birds and went to Emain Macha to lure Conor and the Ulstermen here."

Bricriu hastened back to tell the news to Conor. The king was delighted when he heard Bricriu's story, and they all hurried to Lugh's mansion. When they arrived Dechtire was not there because she had retired to give birth to a baby, but Lugh gave them a hearty welcome and they settled for the night. In the morning Lugh was gone, but Dechtire and her newborn son sat in the middle of the room, and gathered around her were the fifty girls who had been spirited away from Emain Macha.

The whole company knew that this child, the son of Lugh, was destined to become a great hero, so they took counsel with each other about how he should be raised.

Conor said the child should be fostered to Finnchoem, Dechtire's sister, and Finnchoem was delighted to be chosen. But the other champions objected to this, for they, too, wanted to have a hand in rearing the child.

"We will never be able to judge between ourselves!" said Sencha the Wise. "So let Finnchoem take care of the child until we reach Emain Macha, then Morann can judge between our claims."

Off they set for Ulster and when they arrived there, Morann pronounced the following judgment: "You, Conor, will be his special patron, for he is your sister's child. Finnchoem can feed him, Sencha can make an orator out of him, and Blai can provide for his material needs. Fergus can be like a father to him, and Amergin like a brother. This child is destined for greatness. He will be praised by warriors, sages, and kings. He will be a hero to many. He will be the champion of Ulster and defend her rivers and fords. He will fight her battles and avenge her wrongs!"

Finnchoem and Amergin took the child to Dun Breth to a house made of oak. Dechtire, his mother, married Sualdam Mac Roich, and they helped to rear the child as well. He was guided by his fosterers, who taught him their special arts, and he was given the name Setanta.

When he was six years old, Setanta heard about the boy corps that Conor

Mac Nessa had established at Emain Macha. This group of youths was highly skilled with javelin, spear, and sword, and excelled at games, especially hurling. Setanta was determined to join the troop, so despite his mother's objections he made his way to Emain Macha. At first the boys would not accept him because he was too young, but Setanta proved himself so fierce and fearless that he was allowed to join their ranks.

One day when Setanta was seven, Culann, a smith, came to Emain Macha to offer hospitality to the king. "I am not rich," he told Conor, "I have no lands or inherited wealth. Everything I own I earned myself with my tongs and anvil. I want to honor you by welcoming you to my fort, but I beg you to limit your guests so that I can provide enough food for the feast." So the king picked only the most famous and powerful of his household to go with him to Culann's feast.

Before he set out, Conor went to visit the boy corps in the field, where they were playing games. He arrived in time to see Setanta play against all the 150 boys and beat them. While he watched, they changed to shooting goals. Setanta put every ball past the troop and then, in goal alone, stopped every ball that his companions drove at him.

Finally he wrestled with the whole troop and tumbled them all. Conor was amazed at the boy's prowess and he realized what a great

champion Setanta would make. He went over to the boy and said to him, "I'm going to a feast tonight with some of my most prestigious followers. I would like you, Setanta, to come, too, as an honored guest."

"I want to finish the game first," the boy replied. "When I've played enough, I'll follow after you." The king accepted this answer and set off with his followers for Culann's fort.

When they arrived they were greeted by the smith and brought to the hall where the feast had been laid out. Culann said to Conor, "Is all your party present? Or is there someone else still to come?"

"No one," replied the king, forgetting about Setanta.

"Then I'll let loose the hound," the smith said. "He's a savage animal that I got from Spain, and it takes three chains to hold him back, with three men hanging on to each chain. But he guards my stock and cattle well. I'll shut the gate of the enclosure now and let the animal free outside the walls."

The fierce hound was let loose and it made a swift turn around the fortifications of Culann's house. Then it lay down on a hummock, where it could keep watch on the whole place. It crouched there, its giant head on its paws, savage and vigilant, ready to spring.

At Emain Macha, Setanta and the other boys played until it was time to disperse, and then Setanta set out alone for Culann's stronghold. He shortened his journey by hitting the ball with the hurley stick, throwing the stick after the ball, then racing so fast that he caught them both before they fell.

When the monstrous hound saw the boy racing over the green, it let out a bloodcurdling howl that rolled and echoed across the plain. All who heard it froze with horror, but Setanta didn't break his stride. The hound leaped forward, its massive jaws wide open, to tear the child apart.

As it did so, Setanta hurled the ball with all his strength down its gullet, and the force of the throw was so great that it killed the beast.

The hound's savage roar echoed round the hall, and Conor started up in horror. "It's a tragedy that I came here tonight!" he cried out.

"Why is that?" the warriors asked fearfully.

"Because my sister's son was to follow me here. And the roar of that hound is his death knell!"

When the Ulstermen heard this, they rose like one man and stormed out of the fort, swarming over the ramparts in their haste to find the boy. Fastest of all was Fergus Mac Roi, and he was first to reach Setanta.

He found the boy alive, standing over the dead hound, and, overjoyed, he lifted him onto his shoulders and carried him back to Conor. Fergus placed Setanta on the king's knee while all the Red Branch warriors let out shouts of jubilation.

Culann did not join in the rejoicing; he remained outside, looking sadly down at the huge carcass of his hound. Then he came back into the feasting hall and addressed Conor and his retinue.

"It is *indeed* a tragedy that you came here tonight! And it was my bad luck that I invited you at all. I'm glad that you're still alive, boy, but I am ruined! Without the hound to guard it, my fort will be raided and my flocks will be carried off. He saved us all from danger. Little boy, when you killed that hound, you killed my most valued servant!"

"Don't be angry, Culann!" Setanta said. "I'll make up for it!"

"How will you do that, child?" asked Conor.

"I'll find another hound of the same breed and I'll rear him till he can protect Culann as well as the one I've just killed. In the meantime, I will protect your house and herds. I will guard the whole plain and no one will attack you while I am on duty! I will be Culann's hound!"

"That's a fair settlement," said the king.

"No wise man could do better," said Cathbad, the druid. "And from now on, Setanta, your name must be Cuchulainn, the Hound of Culann!"

"I prefer my own name. I'd rather be called Setanta," the boy protested.

"Don't say that," Cathbad replied. "In days to come the name Cuchulainn will be famous throughout Ireland."

And from that moment on the boy was known as Cuchulainn.

BRICRIU'S FEAST

RICRIU, ONE OF THE FOREMOST OF THE ULSTER WARRIORS, WAS famous for causing strife wherever he went. He was such a famous mischief-maker that he got the nickname Bricriu Poison-Tongue.

It came into Bricriu's head to gather together all the Red Branch chiefs at his fort at Dun Rudraige and have some sport with them, so he set about preparing a great feast. He built a dining hall in the same style as the Red Branch hall at Emain Macha, but surpassed it in magnificence. The king's chair, raised on a balcony, was encrusted with jewels that shone so brightly, they turned night into day, and around it were arranged the twelve seats of the twelve tribes of Ulster. Then Bricriu had a platform made for himself on the same level as the king's throne.

When all the preparations had been made, Bricriu went to Emain Macha to invite Conor and the queen to the feast, and also the principal Ulster champions and their wives. Conor told Bricriu that he would accept the invitation but would only go if his followers were willing to attend the feast as well. As it happened the rest of the Ulster chiefs mistrusted Bricriu, and on their behalf Fergus went to Conor to tell him this.

"We don't want to go," Fergus told the king, "for he will set man against man and by nightfall the dead will outnumber the living."

Bricriu overheard what Fergus said to Conor. "It will be worse for you if you don't go!" he said darkly.

"What will happen if we don't go?" Conor asked.

"I will set warrior against warrior until they kill each other."

"We will not be blackmailed by you!" retorted Conor.

"I will set father against son, mother against daughter, wife against wife, till their very mother's milk turns sour!" Bricriu threatened.

"In that case we'd better go!" said Fergus.

Before they set out, Sencha, the judge, called the Ulster chiefs in council to plan how they might protect themselves, and they decided they must get a guarantee from their host that he would leave the hall as soon as the banquet was ready. Bricriu agreed happily.

They had scarcely left Emain Macha, when Bricriu fell to plotting how to cause bad blood among his guests. He drew alongside Laoghaire the Triumphant and greeted him fulsomely. "Laoghaire," he said, "you are a brave warrior. You are the most senior of all the Ulster champions. Why, then, is it that the champion's portion is not given to you at Emain Macha?"

"It would be if I wanted it!" Laoghaire retorted.

"Believe me, the portion *is* worth having! There's a cauldron big enough to hold three men, and I have filled it with strong wine. By way of food I have a seven-year-old boar that has been fed from birth of the best: fresh milk and fine meal in springtime, curds and sweet milk in the summer, nuts and harvest wheat in autumn, and beef broth during the winter. As well as the boar, there is a seven-year-old bull that has eaten only the sweetest meadow hay and oats. Also a hundred honey-soaked wheat cakes, with a quarter bushel of wheat in each one. And it should all be yours, Laoghaire!"

"It had better be mine or there'll be blood spilt!" Laoghaire exclaimed. And Bricriu went off laughing.

A little while later Bricriu drew close to Conall Cearnach and gave him the same advice. When he felt confident that Conall would fight for his right to the champion's portion, Bricriu made his way to Cuchulainn's side.

"How can anyone deny the hero's portion to you, Cuchulainn? You are the acknowledged champion and darling of Ulster. You have defended her borders. You have fought her enemies single-handed. Everyone knows your achievements surpass theirs, so why is the portion not yours by right?"

As he listened to Bricriu, Cuchulainn grew angrier by the minute. "I swear by the gods of my tribe I'll take the head of anyone who dares to claim the portion ahead of me!" he muttered grimly. Then Bricriu left Cuchulainn and mingled with his guests until they reached Dun Rudraige.

When they arrived there the Ulster visitors settled into their quarters, Conor and his men on one side of the building, the queen and the chieftains' wives on the other. Then they made their way to the banqueting hall, where musicians and players entertained the visitors. When the meal was ready to be served, the host and his wife took leave of their guests as agreed, but at the door of the hall Bricriu turned to the assembly. "The champion's portion is over there!" he announced. "Only the greatest hero deserves it. Make sure it goes to the right man!" With that the couple climbed up to the glass viewing room above the hall.

"Bring the hero's portion to Cuchulainn, where you all know it belongs!" roared Cuchulainn's charioteer. Laoghaire and Conall sprang to their feet and seized their weapons. "He doesn't deserve it," they shouted and leapt across the room to fight. Cuchulainn defended

himself fiercely with his sword and shield. The melee was so violent that one half of the hall blazed like the sun, lit by the sparks from their swords, while the other half was covered in the enamel dust that fell like snow from their shields.

At last, Sencha the judge stood up. "Stop!" he roared above the din. "Two men against one is shameful!" Conall and Laoghaire put down their weapons.

"I'll settle this dispute," Sencha said. "Will you abide by my judgment?"

"We will," agreed the three champions.

"Then the champion's portion will be divided among the whole company tonight, and some other time we will decide who is the greatest of the Ulster heroes."

Peace was restored, and the food and wine was divided equally among all.

Watching these developments from the balcony, Bricriu was dismayed to find his feast proceeding harmoniously and decided it was time to set woman against woman as he had set man against man. He went down and waited outside the door for the women to come out of the hall. First out was Fidelma, the wife of Laoghaire, and Bricriu went down to her side.

"I'm the lucky man tonight to meet someone as distinguished as you, Fidelma!" he said. "The wife of Laoghaire and the daughter of Conor Mac Nessa, the king himself! By virtue of birth, beauty, and intelligence you should take second place to none. I'll let you in on a secret! When the women are returning to the feast, if you are the first to reenter the hall you will be considered first in rank among the Ulster women from now on." Fidelma was flattered and pleased.

Just then Lendabar, wife of Conall, came out of the hall, and Bricriu flattered her and told her the same story.

Finally Bricriu greeted Emer, Cuchulainn's wife, and spoke effusively of her lineage, her beauty, and her learning and of her unquestionable right to be the first lady in Ulster after the queen herself. His blandishment and flattery reached new heights, as did his pleasure, when he noted Emer's determination to be first back in the hall.

The three noblewomen and their retinues strolled about companionably in the evening air beyond the third of the ridges that encircled the feasting hall, each one confident that Bricriu had spoken to her alone. When the time came to return to the feast, they began to walk in step toward the hall. At the third ridge, their progress was stately and serene. By the time they reached the second ridge, their steps had become shorter and quicker. At the

first ridge, all dignity was abandoned and the women hitched their skirts around their waists and ran at full tilt, each one trying to be first through the door.

The clamor that the women made resounded through the hall. The men inside sprang for their weapons, striking at each other in their befuddlement, till Sencha called them to order.

"Stop, put down your swords! This is not the arrival of an army that you hear! These are your own women! This is Bricriu's work. He has set your wives against each other while they were out taking the air. If he gets inside with the women, there will be trouble. Shut the door quickly!"

The doorkeeper slammed the door just as Emer, the fastest of the women, arrived. She shouted to be let in first because she had won the race and deserved a higher place than Lendabar or Fidelma. When they heard Emer say this, Conall and Laoghaire ran to the door to open it for their wives so that they might secure a place above Emer. Conor was alarmed at the prospect of another fight and he ordered the champions to return to their places. When the company was calm again, Sencha told them that it would be a war of words that would settle the matter, not a war of arms.

So outside the door, each wife in turn praised her husband's character and person and paid tribute to his courage, skill, deeds, lineage, and virtue, all of them hoping to out-praise the others. When the three warriors heard their wives praising them in such glowing terms, each was determined that his spouse would be the first to enter the hall and claim the highest rank. Laoghaire and Conall hacked at the wall with their swords to force an entrance for their wives, but Cuchulainn simply wrenched one side of the hall up by the foundations and held it so high that the stars in the sky were visible, and Emer stepped into the hall first. Then Cuchulainn let the building fall with a mighty crash, and the foundations sank seven feet into the ground. Bricriu's balcony dipped and slipped, and he and his wife slid out of it and landed among the hounds in the ditch below. When Bricriu saw his house listing at a crazy angle, he ran inside to protest, but he was in such disarray and so caked with mud that no one recognized him until he started to harangue them.

Though Bricriu had paid dearly for his mischief on this occasion, he had succeeded in sowing the seeds of dissension among the Red Branch heroes, and the quarrel about the champion's portion came up again and again. The three contenders went through many tests and ordeals, and the struggle for succession raged on until it was resolved in a bloody and terrifying way.

One evening Conor and Fergus were presiding over a feast in Emain Macha. Laoghaire was there, but Conall and Cuchulainn were absent. As the feast was ending and darkness was drawing in, a giant figure appeared at the end of the hall. He was a monstrous creature and he terrified the assembly as he lumbered across the room. His yellow eyes were as big as cauldrons, and each finger was as thick as a man's wrist. He wore an old skin tunic and over it a rough brown cloak. In one hand, he carried a cudgel the size of a mature tree, and in the other, an ax so sharp that it sliced the hairs that floated in the wind.

"I have come on a mission," said the giant, "for I know that the Ulstermen are world-famous for their courage, dignity, and magnanimity. I have traveled the world through Africa, Europe, and Asia. But I haven't found a man who will do what I ask, not in Greece, Scythia, or Spain. Will anyone here do what I ask?"

"What is your quest?" Conor asked.

"To find a man who will make a pact with me and keep his word."

"That shouldn't be hard!" the king exclaimed.

"Harder than you think," the giant said, "because I'm looking for a man who will agree to cut off my head tonight and let me cut off his head tomorrow." There was silence in the room.

"Conor and Fergus are exempt because of their status as kings," the giant went on, "but is there anyone else present who will make this pact with me?" Still no one spoke. The giant sighed. "Just as I expected! Where are those who claim the champion's portion? Won't one of those heroes pledge his word? Where is Laoghaire the Triumphant?"

"Here I am!" Laoghaire roared. "And I accept your challenge. Bend down and put your neck on the block! I'll cut off your head!"

"That's easily said, but what about tomorrow night?" asked the giant.

"I'll be here," promised Laoghaire.

The huge man bent down, and with one blow of the ax, Laoghaire cut off his head, burying the blade in the block. A torrent of blood flowed across the floor and the head rolled against the wall. Then, to the horror of the crowd, the giant rose, gathered up his head, his axe, and his block and, holding them against his chest, walked out of the room.

The following night, as darkness fell, the giant returned to Emain Macha. His head was back in place, and in his hand he held his cudgel, ax, and block. He stared around the room looking for Laoghaire, but Laoghaire was nowhere to be seen. The giant let out a great resigned sigh and issued his challenge once again. This time it was Conall who agreed to the pact. He gave his solemn word that he would be there on the following night, took up the ax and, with one swift stroke, severed the giant's head from the body.

Once more the giant picked up his head and departed.

The next evening, when the giant returned to Red Branch banquet hall, a great crowd had gathered, but Conall was not among them. The giant laughed contemptuously. "Ulstermen, you're no better that the rest for all your talk!" he jeered. Then he spied Cuchulainn in the middle of the throng. "What about the fierce Cuchulainn, the Hound of Ulster?" he roared. "Can he keep a bargain?"

"I want no bargain with you!" Cuchulainn shouted, and he grabbed the ax from the giant's hand and struck off his head with such force that it bounced to the ceiling. When it landed, Cuchulainn took another crack, but still the giant rose to his feet, took up his shattered head, and left.

On the fourth evening every warrior in Ulster was in the Red Branch hall to see if Cuchulainn would be there. Cuchulainn was indeed present, but he was dejected and frightened and would not speak to anyone.

Suddenly the giant appeared at the far end of the hall. "Where is Cuchulainn?" he demanded.

"Here I am," Cuchulainn answered in a low voice.

"You haven't as much to say for yourself tonight!" mocked the giant. "I can see you are scared to die! But at least you have kept your word." The giant pointed to the block, and Cuchulainn knelt down and laid his head on it.

"Stretch out your neck!" the giant ordered.

"Kill me quickly and don't torment me," Cuchulainn begged.

"Your neck is too short for the block!"

"Then I'll make it as long as a heron's neck!" Cuchulainn cried and he distorted his body and stretched his neck till it reached across the block. Using both hands, the giant swung the ax so high that it struck the rafters. The swish of his cloak through the air and the hiss of the ax as it came down sounded through the hall like the wind through trees on a stormy night. As the crowd watched helplessly, the ax swung down toward Cuchulainn's neck, but it was the blunt side of the blade that landed there and it came down so gently that it hardly marked the skin.

"Stand up, Cuchulainn!" the giant said. "You are the champion of Ulster. No one is your equal for bravery and honor. From now on your supremacy must go unchallenged. You must be awarded the champion's portion, and your wife must take first place after the queen in the banqueting hall. I am Cu Roi and I swear by the oath of my people that whomever disputes this puts his life in danger!" With that, the giant disappeared.

DEIRDRE OF THE SORROWS

N IRELAND, LONG AGO, EVERY CHIEFTAIN'S HOUSEHOLD HAD its own bard who entertained the company with songs and poetry and praised the heroic deeds of his master. The bards in turn were held in high esteem, and Felimid, the bard of the king of Ulster, held an important place within the clan.

One day Felimid invited the king to his house and prepared a lavish feast in his honor. The guests ate and drank their fill, and the hall was full of the sounds of entertainment. Felimid's wife oversaw the feast, moving among the guests the whole night long, until at last they began to fall asleep. Then she made her way to her own room, for her baby was about to be born. As she passed through the house, the child in her womb gave a shriek so loud that the warriors seized their weapons and rushed to see what had made the unearthly cry. Nobody could say what it was till Felimid came from his wife's chamber and told them.

Then Felimid's wife emerged distraught and frightened. She turned to Cathbad the Druid and said, "You are a wise and generous man, and you can foretell the future. Can you please tell me what lies inside my womb?"

The druid answered, "The infant that screamed from your womb is a girl. She will grow up to be a beautiful woman. She will have shining eyes and long, heavy, fair hair. Her pale skin will be flushed with pink, her lips will be as red as strawberries, and she will have teeth like pearls. Queens will envy her, and kings will desire her. She will be known as Deirdre of the Sorrows, and because of her, there will be great anguish in Ulster!"

"Kill the child," the warriors shouted, "so that Ulster may be spared!"

But Conor Mac Nessa held up his hand. "No!" he said, "I will take this child and foster her to someone I trust, and when she grows up she will be my wife."

No one dared argue with the king. He built a fort for Deirdre in a lonely place, and she grew more beautiful each day. But apart from the king himself, the only people to see her beauty were her foster father and Levercham, her nurse.

One winter's day Deirdre's foster father was slaughtering a calf for veal and the blood flowed out across the snow. As Deirdre watched from her window a raven swooped down to sip the blood. Deirdre turned to Levercham and said, "I could love a man like that, a man with hair as black as a raven and skin like the snow and cheeks as red as blood!"

"Good luck is yours," Levercham answered, "for not far from here lives such a man. He is called Naoise, and he is one of the sons of Usnach. These three brothers are so courageous and skillful that, back to back, they can hold off all the warriors in Ulster. They are so swift that they can take down deer like hunting dogs. And when they sing together their song is so harmonious that women and men, entranced by the music, fall silent. Ardan, Ainnle, and Naoise, these are their names, but Naoise is the strongest and most handsome of the three."

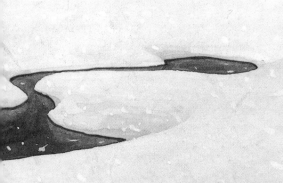

"If that is so," said Deirdre, "I will not have a day's good health till I see him!"

Not long after this, when spring had come to Emain Macha, Deirdre heard melodious singing coming from the ramparts of the fort. She stole out, for she knew that it must be Naoise. She walked past him without glancing in his direction, but Naoise saw her, and was so struck by her beauty, that he stopped in the middle of his song and he shouted out, "This is a fine young lassie passing me by!"

"Lasses are bound to be fine when there are no lads about!" Deirdre retorted.

"You have the king for yourself!" said Naoise, realizing that the beautiful girl must be Deirdre.

Deirdre looked at Naoise. "If I had my choice between a fine young fellow like yourself and an old man like Conor, I would settle for you!"

"But you are promised to the king," said Naoise. "And don't forget what Cathbad has prophesied about you!"

"Are you turning me down?" Deirdre shouted.

"I am indeed!" replied Naoise.

In a fit of passion, Deirdre ran up to Naoise and, grabbing his head between her hands, she cried, "May dishonor and disgrace fall on this head unless you take me away with you!"

Naoise was stricken with dread when he heard these words and realized that Deirdre had put a *geis*, a most solemn bond, on him. He knew that to disobey that *geis* would bring about his downfall, so, terrified as he was of Conor Mac Nessa's anger, he knew he must take Deirdre with him. That night, as darkness fell, Deirdre and the sons of Usnach fled from the province of Ulster.

For a while they wandered around Ireland going from one king's protection to another's, but they were harried again and again by Conor's men. In the end, they could stand it no longer and left Ireland for Scotland.

There they set up camp among the wild mountains and glens and lived on the game they caught. When winter came and the game was scarce, they stole cattle for food. These cattle raids angered the people of the place, who marched on Naoise's compound to kill him and his followers. The sons of Usnach, seeing the men advance, fled to the king of Scotland and offered to fight for him in exchange for food and sanctuary. The king was glad to have such fine soldiers as allies and took them into his service. Because they remembered Cathbad's warning that Deirdre's beauty would bring about death and destruction, Naoise and his followers built their houses in a circle with a secret house for Deirdre in the center.

But early one morning the king's steward rose and stole into the brothers' quarters. There he found the secret hut and Naoise and Deirdre asleep in it. Like everyone else who saw her, he was mesmerized by the girl's beauty and he ran in great excitement to tell the king.

"Until this day we have never found anyone worthy to be your queen, but now I have found a woman worthy to be queen of the whole world! Kill Naoise while he's still asleep and make the woman your wife!"

"I won't do that," the king said. "We'll try a different way. Every day when Naoise is out, go to the girl's room and tell her that the king of Scotland loves her. Ask her to leave Naoise and come here to be my wife." So every day, in secret, the steward wooed Deirdre for the king and every night when Naoise returned, Deirdre told him the whole story.

Then the king arranged dangerous missions for the three brothers, hoping that they would be killed, but their skill and bravery brought them through unharmed. At last the king gave Deirdre an ultimatum: Either she come to him voluntarily, or she would be taken by force and the three brothers killed.

Deirdre warned Naoise of the danger. "We must leave immediately," she urged, "or by nightfall tomorrow you and your brothers will be dead!" That night, the whole party stole away in boats and headed for a remote island from where they could see both Ireland and Scotland. When the news reached Ireland, the Red Branch warriors went to Conor. "This is Deirdre's

doing, not theirs," they told him. "It would be tragic if the sons of Usnach were killed in a foreign land because of a headstrong woman. You should forgive them."

"Let them come back, then," the king said, "and tell them I will send someone to guarantee their safe passage."

The fugitives were delighted. They sent a message back to Conor thanking him for his pardon and requesting him to send the champions Fergus, Dubhtach, and Cormac. Conor agreed to this, but there was treachery in his heart. He still wanted Deirdre for himself.

Conor knew that there was a geis on Fergus that he must never, under pain of death, refuse to attend a feast that had been prepared in his honor, and he used that knowledge to trick Fergus. He ordered him to bring Deirdre, Naoise, and their household directly to Emain Macha as soon as they arrived in Ireland and on no account to eat or drink anywhere until they had eaten and drunk with him. Then he ordered Borrach, a chief whose

house lay on the route to Emain Macha, to prepare a feast in Fergus's honor. When Fergus arrived at Borrach's stronghold, the chieftain did as the king had ordered and invited him to the feast. At first Fergus declined the invitation, but when Borrach assured him that the feast was in his honor and reminded him of his geis, Fergus turned pale. "It is a cruel choice!" he shouted. "I have given my word to accompany Naoise and Deirdre to Emain Macha without delay but I cannot refuse your hospitality, unwelcome as it is!"

Naoise and Deirdre were alarmed. "Are you forsaking us for a meal?"

"I'm not forsaking you," Fergus said, "but I cannot betray my geis. I'll send my son, Fiacha, with you to ensure your safe conduct." So Deirdre and the sons of Usnach set off for Emain Macha while Fergus, Cormac, and Dubtach went to Borrach's feast.

When the travelers arrived at Emain Macha another band of visitors was already with Conor. They were led by Eogan, whose father, the king of Fernmag, had been a long-standing enemy of Conor's. Eogan had come to make peace with the king of Ulster, and Conor, seizing his chance, had accepted his offer on condition that he kill the sons of Usnach.

As Deirdre and the brothers stood on the green at the center of Emain Macha, Eogan of Fernmag began to move toward the sons of Usnach. Fergus's son, Fiacha, sensing danger, went up to stand beside Naoise. As Eogan came close, Naoise went to greet him. In reply, Eogan drew his sword and drove it through Naoise's body. As Naoise fell, Fiacha caught him in his arms and pulled him down to shield him with his body, but Eogan killed Naoise through the body of Fiacha.

Then Conor's mercenaries closed in on Ainnle, Ardan, and their followers. They hunted them like hares from one end of the green to the other and killed them all. Deirdre was seized, her hands were tied behind her back, and she was handed over to Conor.

When Fergus heard of Conor's treachery he was mad with anger, and for sixteen years, he and his allies made raids on Conor Mac Nessa's territory. In revenge, Deirdre was kept in Conor's house for a year. In all that time she was never once seen to smile or laugh. She hardly slept at all, and the little food she ate barely kept her alive.

When Conor brought musicians to play for her, she would not listen to their songs. Instead she raised her voice and recited a poem lamenting Naoise's death. When the king tried to win her favor, she accused him bitterly of Naoise's murder and threw his love back in his face. Conor grew more and more enraged at Deirdre's defiance and at her rejection of him.

One day when Eogan was visiting Emain Macha, Conor brought him to see Deirdre. Then the king asked her. "Of all that you see, Deirdre, what do you hate most?"

"I hate you, Conor, and I hate Eogan who killed Naoise," Deirdre answered.

"In that case you can spend a year with him as well!" said Conor, and he handed her over to Eogan.

The next day the three of them drove out to the fair at Emain Macha. Deirdre was in the chariot between Eogan and Conor and throughout the journey she kept her eyes fixed on the ground, for she had vowed that she would not look at either of the men. Seeing this, Conor taunted her. "Well, Deirdre, here you are where you can eye us both, like a ewe between two rams!"

They were galloping past a huge boulder when Conor spoke these mocking words, and hearing them, Deirdre could bear her fate no longer. She leapt out of the chariot to escape her tormentors, fell against the rock, and died.

THE FINN CYCLE

ong ago, a band of men called the Fianna roamed through Ireland. This troop was made up of the noblest, bravest, swiftest, strongest, most honorable men in the land. From November to May, the Fianna were the soldiers of the king. They kept the country safe from pirates and invaders and punished public enemies at home. In the summer months, they received no pay, but lived off the land, fishing and hunting for food and selling the skins of animals.

To be accepted as one of the Fianna, a man had to obey certain rules and prove himself in trials of strength, bravery, and skill. He had to swear to be loyal to his leader, to respect all women, and to help the poor. He had to study the art of poetry so he could compose his own poems and memorize traditional rhymes and stories. When he had pledged all these things, his comrades-in-arms tested his courage and skill. If he came through these trials as a bravehearted warrior, a lightfooted hunter, and an eloquent poet, he was allowed to join the company.

The captain of the Fianna had great power and sat next to the king at the banquet table. Finn Mac Cumhaill of Clan Bascna was the most famous leader of them all, and during his time, they had a heyday of such glory that the stories of their adventures were told all over Ireland from that day on.

FINN AND THE SALMON OF KNOWLEDG

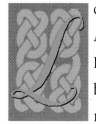ONG AGO IN IRELAND, A DRUID LIVED ON THE HILL OF Allen in Leinster, in a shining, white-fronted fort called Almu. His name was Tadg and he had a daughter, Muirne, who was so beautiful that the sons of kings and chiefs came in great numbers to ask for her hand. Among her suitors was Cumhaill, head of Clan Bascna and leader of the Fianna. Cumhaill asked Tadg for permission to marry his daughter again and again, but each time he was refused. In spite of these refusals Cumhaill was determined to have Muirne for his wife, so he entered the fort of Almu and carried her off.

When the druid heard that his daughter had been abducted, he was furious and went directly to the king and complained bitterly. Conn sent messengers to Cumhaill ordering him to send Muirne back to her father, but Cumhaill refused. He told the king that he would give him anything he asked, anything at all, except Muirne. When Conn heard this defiant reply, he gathered together from the east and the west the chiefs and soldiers of Clan Morna, the great rivals of Clan Bascna. From the south, bands of men loyal to Clan Bascna marched to Leinster to help Cumhaill. The two armies met at Cnuca, near Castleknock, and a fierce battle ensued. Cumhaill fought bravely leading his small force against Conn's bigger army, but he was overpowered and killed, and only a few of his men escaped alive. After the battle the king rewarded the leader of Clan Morna by putting him at the head of the Fianna.

When Muirne heard that her husband had been killed in battle and his followers scattered, she went back to Almu to seek refuge with her father, but Tadg was so angry with her for eloping with Cumhaill that he turned her away from his door. Muirne made her way to the king's fortress at Tara

and asked Conn for his protection, not only
from Clan Morna, but from her father as
well. The king took pity on her, and
one of his servants brought her to a
kinsman's house, where she was kept
in hiding. Not long afterward she
gave birth to a boy, the son of
Cumhaill, and she called him
Demne.

While he was a baby, Demne
had no home where he could
be safe. Goll Mac Morna, the
new leader, was determined
to kill him for he was afraid
that Cumhaill's son would
claim his position as leader
of the Fianna when he grew
up. Muirne knew that her
son was in danger while he
was with her, so, with a sad
heart, she handed him
over to two of her trust-
ed women attendants,
skilled trackers who had
been trained to survive
in the wilderness.

As soon as Muirne's servants were given the baby, they took him away with them, and hid with him in the woods and valleys of Slieve Bloom. There they guarded him closely and reared him and and cared for him as if he were their own child. Muirne slipped away out of the territory controlled by Clan Morna and settled in the south of the country.

Six years after she had parted with her child, Muirne came secretly to visit Demne in his forest hideout. She wanted to see her son again and make sure he was hidden from his enemies and well cared for by his friends. Demne lived in a hunting bothy made of wattle and mud and roofed with branches, so that it was almost invisible in the depths of the wood, but Muirne found it and went in. Her two women servants recognized her and welcomed her joyfully. They led her into the room where her fair-haired son lay asleep. She lifted him up and, holding him close, hugged him and talked to him. Then rocking him in her arms she sang him a lullaby until he went back to sleep. When he was sound asleep, Muirne whispered good-bye to her son and went out of the room. She thanked the faithful women for the love and protection they were giving her child and asked them to look after him until he was old enough to fend for himself. Then she stole away, slipping from wood to wilderness till she reached the safety of her own territory.

As Demne grew up, his guardians taught him to love the changing seasons and life in the woods and hills around him, and he grew up out of doors, hardy in winter and carefree in summer. He became a skillful tracker and hunter; he could outstrip the hare, and bring down a stag on his own without the help of a deerhound, and he could make a wild duck drop from the sky with one stone from a sling.

As he became more and more adventurous, Demne went farther and farther afield, in spite of the warnings of his guardians, and before long word came to Goll Mac Morna of a fair-haired forest boy. One day Demne came out of the woods onto the playing green of a large fort. There were boys playing hurley on the green, and Demne joined in the game and was by far the best player of them all. As soon as the game was over, he disappeared into the forest so swiftly the boys scarcely saw him go. The next day he came back, and on his own, played against a quarter of the boys and won. Again he slipped away. The next day, a third of the boys measured themselves against him, but Demne still beat them. Finally they were all ranged against him, but the fair-haired stranger took the ball from them all and won the game.

"What is your name?" the boys asked.

"Demne," he said, and turned away and disappeared into the forest. The boys told the chieftain who owned the fort about the stranger who had beaten them all single-handed.

"Surely among the lot of you, you should be able to beat one boy!" the chieftain said mockingly. "Did he tell you his name?"

"He said his name was Demne."

"And what does this champion look like?"

"He's tall and well-built and his hair is very fair."

"Then we'll give him the nickname Finn because of that white hair," said the chieftain, and from that day on Finn, which means "fair-haired," became Demne's name.

The chieftain's son grew
jealous of Finn's strength and skill
and he turned his companions against
the newcomer. When Finn arrived the next day
ready for a game, instead of playing with him, all the
boys flung their hurley sticks at him. Finn grabbed one of the
hurleys from the ground and made a run at the boys, knocking seven
of them to the ground and scattering the rest. Then he escaped to the
shelter of the forest.

The two women who had guarded Demne so faithfully knew they
could keep him safe no longer, now that tales of his exploits were on
everyone's lips.

"You must leave us, Finn. The Mac Morna scouts will be on your track,
and if they find you, they will kill you," they told him.

Finn sadly said good-bye to his brave guardians and headed out, away
from the dangerous terrain of Slieve Bloom. He traveled south, slipping
stealthily through bogs and woods down the country until he reached
Lough Lene in Kerry.

He made
his way to the stronghold
of the king of Bantry and joined his band of fighters
and trackers, but he told no one his name or lineage. Before long, it was
clear to all that the newcomer had no equal as a hunter, and was a skilled
chess player as well. The king observed the young man closely and saw in
his face a resemblance to Cumhaill, his father.

"Who are you?" he demanded.

"I'm called Demne," replied Finn.

"No, you are not! You're the son of Cumhaill. You are called Finn Mac Cumhaill, and your mother was Muirne, the druid's daughter. Goll Mac Morna killed your father at Castleknock and now he is out to kill you, too! Leave my place at once. I can't protect you!"

So once again Finn was a fugitive, and he decided to seek refuge with his uncle Crimhall. Finn felt safe in the company of loyal kinsmen, and he listened closely to the old man's stories about Cumhaill and the Fianna. As Crimhall told him about their bravery in battle, their skill in the hunt, and their mastery of the art of poetry, Finn made up his mind to overthrow Goll Mac Morna and take his hereditary place at the head of the Fianna. But he knew that he must gather around him a band of men. He knew, too, that he would not be considered worthy to take command of the Fianna until he was as fine a poet as he was a warrior and hunter.

Now there was a poet and teacher called Finnegas who lived near the river Boyne, and Finn decided to learn the art of poetry from this wise man. Finnegas had spent seven years camping near a pool on the river Boyne because the red-speckled Salmon of Knowledge lived in this pool and it had been foretold that whoever ate one of these fish would possess an understanding of everything in the world, past, present, and future. The salmon had eaten the berries that fell from a magic rowan tree overhanging the pool, and from the berries they had absorbed all the wisdom of the world.

When Finn arrived at Finnegas's hut, the poet had just caught one of the salmon and knew that, at last, all the knowledge of the world would be his.

Finnegas gave the fish to Finn and ordered him to cook it, but he gave the youth a solemn warning not to taste even the smallest morsel. Finn

made a fire and cooked the salmon, but as he lifted it off the spit, the charred skin of the fish seared his thumb. The burn made Finn wince, and he stuck his blistered thumb into his mouth to ease the pain. Then he brought the fish to Finnegas. As Finn handed him the fish, the poet looked closely at his pupil and saw a change in him.

"Are you sure you didn't taste the salmon?" he asked the boy anxiously.

"No," said Finn, "but I burnt my thumb on the skin of the fish and put it in my mouth to soothe it."

"What is your name?" the poet cried.

"My name is Demne," the boy replied.

"Your name is Finn!" said the poet sadly. "As mine is too. It was prophesied that a fair-haired man would eat the Salmon of Knowledge, and you are that fair-haired one, not me! So the eternal knowledge is yours now, not mine. You may as well eat the whole fish, Finn!"

So Finn ate the Salmon of Knowledge and from that moment on when he put his thumb in his mouth, whatever he needed to know was revealed to him.

Finn stayed with Finnegas on the banks of the Boyne, learning the art of poetry, and to prove that he had mastered that difficult art, he composed his first poem in praise of early summer, the season he loved best of all.

SUMMER

EARLY SUMMER, LOVELIEST SEASON,
THE WORLD IS BEING COLORED IN.
WHILE DAYLIGHT LASTS ON THE HORIZON,
SUDDEN, THROATY BLACKBIRDS SING.

THE DUSTY-COLORED CUCKOO CUCKOOS.
"WELCOME, SUMMER" IS WHAT HE SAYS.
WINTER'S UNIMAGINABLE.
THE WOOD'S A WICKERWORK OF BOUGHS.

SUMMER MEANS THE RIVER'S SHALLOW,
THIRSTY HORSES NOSE THE POOLS.
LONG HEATHER SPREADS OUT ON BOG PILLOWS.
WHITE BOG COTTON DROOPS IN BLOOM.

SWALLOWS SWERVE AND FLICKER UP.
MUSIC STARTS BEHIND THE MOUNTAIN.
THERE'S MOSS AND A LUSH GROWTH UNDERFOOT.
SPONGY MARSHLAND GLUGS AND STUTTERS.

BOG BANKS SHINE LIKE RAVENS' WINGS.
THE CUCKOO KEEPS ON CALLING WELCOME.
THE SPECKLED FISH JUMPS; AND THE STRONG
SWIFT WARRIOR IS UP AND RUNNING.

A LITTLE, JUMPY, CHIRPY FELLOW
HITS THE HIGHEST NOTE THERE IS;
THE LARK SINGS OUT HIS CLEAR TIDINGS.
SUMMER, SHIMMER, PERFECT DAYS.

THE ENCHANTED DEER

NE FINE DAY WHEN FINN MAC CUMHAILL AND HIS MEN were returning home after a day's hunting, a beautiful deer started up in front of them and began to run as fast as the wind toward the fort of Almu. The doe ran with such speed that she outstripped the hunting party, and one by one the men and their dogs fell back exhausted. But Finn and his two hounds kept up the chase. As they swept along the side of a valley, the deer was still in view but she was outstripping Bran and Sceolan, the swiftest dogs in the pack, and Finn knew he would never be able to overtake her. Suddenly, in full flight, she stopped and lay down on the smooth grass. Finn was amazed at this strange behavior and he ran on toward her, Bran and Sceolan ahead of him. When Finn came close to the beautiful doe he was even more astonished to see his two fierce deerhounds frolicking around her, licking her face and neck and patting her limbs.

Finn knew by this that no harm should come to the deer, so he called his dogs to heel and they set off for the Hill of Allen, where Almu stood. After they had walked a little distance Finn looked behind him, and there, on their heels, was the doe following them home. When they reached the fort, Finn and his hounds went through the entrance, and their strange companion followed them. Everyone knew then that this was no ordinary deer, and she was given safe quarters for the night.

After the evening meal Finn retired to his room. Just as he lay down, a lovely woman walked in, dressed in clothes of the finest material, richly ornamented with gold. Finn stared at the visitor in surprise, for he knew she was not a member of the household, and in admiration, because she was so beautiful. Then the woman spoke.

"I am the doe you and your hounds spared this evening and brought safely back to Almu. I am called Sadb. A druid of the Tuatha De Danaan, the Dark Druid, changed me into a deer because I refused his love. For three years now I have endured the hardship and danger of a wild deer's life in a part of Ireland far away from here. In the end, one of the druid's servants took pity and told me that if I could get inside a Fianna fortress, the druid's power over me would come to an end. I have been running through the woods of Ireland without stopping so that I could come close to the Hill of Allen, for I knew you were the leader of the Fianna. I outran your hunting party until Bran and Sceolan were my only pursuers. Then I stopped, for I knew they wouldn't kill me. They recognized my true nature, which is like their own."

Finn was moved by the woman's story and by her gentleness and beauty, and he fell deeply in love with her. For months he abandoned all his former activities and was not seen at any hunt, fight, or feast. Instead he stayed with his beloved Sadb and he gave her a pet name, the Flower of Almu.

But word came to Almu from the king, who needed Finn's help to drive invaders out of Dublin Bay, so Finn had to leave Almu and beautiful Sadb.

For seven days Finn was away, driving back the Lochlann from the Irish coast. The moment the battle was over, he hurried back to the Hill of Allen.

When the shining walls of Almu came into view, his eyes scoured the ramparts for his first glimpse of Sadb. He came closer and closer, his eyes

straining anxiously to see his wife, but there was no sign of her anywhere.

Instead of Sadb, his servants came out to meet him. They cheered his safe return, but their faces were sad.

"Where is Sadb?" Finn cried out. No one spoke, for no one wanted to be the first to break the bad news. "Where is my wife?" Finn asked again.

"Don't blame us, Finn!" his servants implored. "While you were away fighting the invaders, you appeared here outside the fort with Bran and Sceolan at your heels. You put the pipes to your lips, and its humming music filled Almu, mesmerizing and soothing us all. Sadb, your gentle wife, at once came running out of her room, thinking you had returned. She flew down through the pass and out toward the gates of Almu. By then we knew that it was not you who was blowing the pipes, but someone who had assumed your shape, but Sadb ignored our entreaties. 'I must go out to greet Finn! He has saved and protected me! And now I am carrying his child.' We begged her to stay inside the fort, but she ran out of Almu and threw herself into the arms of the one who had taken on your shape. Immediately she realized her mistake. She gave a wild shriek and drew back, but the sorcerer struck her with a wand. In an instant Sadb was gone, and a beautiful, frightened deer stood in her place. The doe stood trembling on the plain, looking back piteously toward Almu. Then the druid's two hounds, barking wildly, chased the terrified deer away from the fort. Three or four times she made

desperate efforts to spring back across the fortifications, but each time the hounds seized her by the throat and pulled her back.

"Oh, Finn!" they cried, seeing the grief and horror on his face. "We swear to you that we tried our best to save Sadb. Before you could count to twenty we had snatched our spears and swords and rushed out to the plain to rescue her, but the plain was deserted. We could see nothing, no sign of woman or deer, man or hound. Nothing! But we could hear the beat of running feet drumming the plain, and the howl of dogs. These sounds filled the air all around us and bewildered us, for each of us heard the sounds coming from a different direction."

Finn threw his head back in anguish when he heard this and hammered his breast with his fists. He uttered not one word but went alone to his quarters, and there he stayed the rest of that day and night and wasn't seen by anyone till dawn broke the next day over the Liffey plain.

For fourteen years after that, Finn searched the country, exploring the remotest corners of the land in search of his beloved Sadb. All that time his face was sad, and he was never seen to smile. Except in the heat of battle or the excitement of a chase, his spirits never lifted. When he went hunting he left his main pack of dogs behind and took with him only Bran and Sceolan and three other hounds that he could trust. He wanted to be sure that Sadb would be left unharmed, if by good chance they ever found her.

Fourteen years after Sadb had been taken away, Finn and the Fianna were hunting on the side of Ben Bulben in Sligo when they heard the loud baying of the hounds ahead of them in a narrow pass. They rushed to the place to see what the clamor was about and found Finn's five hounds forming a circle round a naked youth whose long hair reached almost to his feet.

Finn's hounds were fighting furiously to hold back the rest of the pack as they tried to seize the boy. The youth stood calmly at the center of the circle, unconcerned by the turbulent dogfight that surged around his feet. He stared curiously at the men of the Fianna as they hurried to rescue him. As soon as the other dogs had been called off, Bran and Sceolan turned to the wild boy and whined and yelped at him, licking his face and limbs and jumping up on him as if he, and not Finn, were their master. Finn and his companions went up to the handsome youth and stroked his head gently and hugged him to show him he would not be harmed. They brought him with them to their hunting bothy and gave him food and drink.

When they returned to Almu, the youth came with them and there they gave him clothes and cut his hair, and gradually he began to be easy in their company and forgot his sudden, wild ways. Finn, staring intently at the boy, saw in his features a shadow of the lovely face of Sadb. He judged him to be about fourteen years of age, the number of years since Sadb had been spirited away, and he felt sure that the woodland boy was their child. Finn loved the youth and kept him at his side all day long. He talked to him and told him stories, and the boy learned to speak. Like their master, Bran and Sceolan loved their new companion and spent all their time playing around him, waiting to be petted. When the boy had learned to speak, he told Finn this story.

"It was a deer, a gentle doe, who protected me and sheltered me when I was a child. She cared for me night and day, and I loved her like a mother. We lived in a wild, lonely place, a mountain park, surrounded by high peaks and sheer cliffs. We stayed together all the time, ranging through valleys, over rocky slopes, drinking from the streams, hiding in the dark woods. We roamed through every corner of the region till we knew each hill and glen, but though we were free to wander where we liked in our mountain home, we were prisoners there. We couldn't escape because of the mountains and cliffs that circled it. During the summer we fed on berries and fruit, for there were plenty of them in the woods and hedges, and in the winter, provisions were left for me in a sheltered cave.

"A dark-haired man visited us from time to time. He would talk to the doe. Sometimes he spoke gently to her, sometimes he shouted at her in a loud, threatening voice, but no matter how he spoke to her, she shrank away from him with terrified eyes, every limb quivering with fear. The man could not get near her and he always left in a great rage.

"One day this man, the Dark Druid, arrived when we were beside a high cliff. He came close to the doe and spoke to her. At first he spoke tenderly to her, coaxing her to come away with him. Then he harangued her, threatening her in a loud, harsh voice. He kept this treatment up for a long time, but the doe still shrank away out of his reach, trembling and shaking. Suddenly the Dark Druid moved close to the doe, cornering her in a narrow place, and took a hazel

wand and struck her with it. He cast a spell on her, and she was powerless then to do anything except follow him. As the druid led her away, she kept looking back at me, bleating and calling out with heartbroken cries. I was sobbing, too, and I made desperate attempts to follow her but try as I might, I could not move a limb for I, too, had been put under a spell. I was frightened and lonely and I shouted out again and again, but I could do nothing but listen to the deer's cries grow fainter and more desperate as she was taken away. In the end I was so overcome with sadness that I fainted and fell to the ground.

"When I woke up, the hilly region where the doe and I had lived so happily had gone, and I found myself in a place I had never seen before. I searched for days for the high mountains and familiar cliffs, but I couldn't find them anywhere. I wandered alone exploring the new terrain for a few more days until I heard the baying of the hounds as they picked up my scent in the mountain pass. Bran and Sceolan protected me till you, Finn, and the men of the Fianna arrived and brought me here to Almu."

When Finn heard this story he was happy, for he knew for certain that the youth was his child and the child of his beloved Sadb, and he called the boy Oisin, which means "Little Deer."

OISIN IN THE LAND OF YOUTH

UNDREDS OF YEARS AFTER FINN MAC CUMHAILL AND HIS companions had died, Saint Patrick came to Ireland and brought with him the Christian religion. As he traveled around the country preaching the gospel, he heard many stories about the adventures of Finn and the Fianna, and he became interested in these old heroes. Their story seemed to be written into the very landscape of Ireland; hills and woods resounded with their legends, rivers and valleys bore their names, dolmens marked their graves.

One day a feeble, blind old man was brought to Patrick. Patrick preached the new doctrines to him, but the old warrior defiantly sang the praises of the Fianna, their code of honor and their way of life. He said he was Oisin, the son of Finn himself.

Patrick doubted the old man's word, since Finn and his followers had been dead longer than the span of any human life. So to convince the saint that his claim was true, Oisin, the last of the Fianna, told this story:

The Battle of Gowra was the last battle that Finn and the Fianna ever fought. When it was over, only a handful of survivors were left, among them Finn and his son, Oisin. This little band escaped from the battlefield and made their way south to Lough Lene in Kerry, a favorite haunt of theirs in happier times.

One May morning, when the early mists were beginning to lift over the fresh, green woods around Lough Lene, Finn and his followers set out to hunt. The beauty of the countryside and the prospect of the chase revived their spirits a little as they followed the hounds through the woods. Suddenly a young, hornless deer broke cover and bounded through the forest with the dogs in full cry at its heels. The Fianna followed them, rejuvenated by the familiar excitement of the chase.

As they headed toward the coast, they were stopped in their tracks by the sight of a lovely young woman galloping toward them on a nimble white horse. She was as beautiful as a vision. Her eyes were as clear and blue as the May sky, and they sparkled like the dew on the bluebells at her feet. Around the horse's head and neck hung a golden bridle, and the shoes on its hooves were made of gold. In all their lives the Fianna had never seen a finer animal.

The woman approached. "I've traveled a great distance to find you," she said.

"Who are you and where have you come from?" Finn asked, moonstruck.

"I am called Niamh of the Golden Hair, and my father is the king of Tir na n-Og, the Land of Youth." the girl replied.

"Has tragedy brought you here?"

"No," she answered. "I came because I love your son."

Finn started in surprise. "You love one of my sons?"

"Oisin is the one," replied Niamh. "Reports of his handsome looks and sweet nature reached even as far as the Land of Youth, so I decided to come and find him."

Oisin had been silent all this time. But now he recovered himself. "You are the most beautiful woman in the world," he said, "and I would choose you above all others. I will gladly marry you!"

"Come away with me, Oisin!" Niamh whispered. "Come back with me to the Land of Youth. You will never fall ill or grow old there; you will never die. Trees grow tall there, and all year round the branches bow low with fruit. The land flows with honey and wine, as much as you could ever want. In Tir na n-Og you will sit at feasts and games, and there will be plenty of music for you, plenty of wine. You will have more gold than you could imagine, and a hundred swords, a hundred silk tunics, a hundred swift bay horses, a hundred keen hunting dogs. The king of the Ever Young will place a crown on your head, a crown that he has never given to anyone else, and it will protect you from every danger. As well as all of this, you will get beauty, strength, and power. And me for your wife."

"Oh, Niamh, I could never refuse you anything you ask." cried Oisin, and he jumped up on the horse behind her.

"Go slowly, Oisin, until we reach the shore!" Niamh cautioned.

When Finn saw his son being borne away from him toward the sea, he let out three loud, sorrowful shouts.

Oisin turned the horse back and dismounted. He embraced his father and said good-bye to all his friends. With tears streaming down his face he took a last look at them as they stood on the shore. He saw the defeat and sadness on his father's face and the sorrow of his friends. He remembered the happy times he had spent with them in the excitement of the chase and the heat of battle. But grief-stricken as he was, he could not stay, and he mounted the horse again and shook the reins. At that, the white horse tossed its mane, gave three shrill neighs, and leapt forward into the sea. The waves opened before Niamh and Oisin and closed behind them as they passed.

As they traveled through the waves, wonderful sights appeared on every side. They passed cities, courts, and castles, whitewashed bawns and forts, painted summerhouses fragrant with flowers, and stately palaces. A young fawn rushed past, a white dog with scarlet ears racing after it. A beautiful young woman on a bay horse galloped by on the crests of the waves, carrying a golden apple in her right hand; behind her rode a young noble-man, handsome and richly dressed with a gold-bladed sword in his hand.

Ahead of them, away in the distance, a shining palace came into view standing serenely on a hillside. Its delicate facade shone in the sun.

"What a handsome palace that is!" Oisin exclaimed. "Who lives there and what is the name of the country he rules?"

"This is the Land of Virtue, and that is the palace of Fomor, a ferocious giant," Niamh replied. "The daughter of the king of the Land of Life is the queen. She was abducted from her own court by Fomor, and he keeps her prisoner here. She has put a spell on him that he may not marry her until a champion has challenged him to single combat. But a prisoner she remains, for no one wants to fight the giant."

"Niamh, even though your voice is music to my ears, the story you have told me is sad," Oisin said. "I'll go to the fortress and try to over-come the giant and set the queen free."

They turned the horse toward the white palace, and when they arrived there they were welcomed by a woman almost as beautiful as Niamh herself. She seated them on golden chairs and, with tears spilling down her cheeks, she told them how much she longed to be free of Fomor.

"Dry your eyes," Oisin told her. "I'll challenge the giant. I'm not afraid of him! Either I'll kill him or I'll fight till he kills me."

At that moment, Fomor came into the castle, and when he saw Oisin, with a loud, angry roar he challenged him to a fight.

For three days and three nights they grappled. Powerful and fierce as Fomor was, Oisin overpowered him in the end and cut off his head. The two women gave three triumphant cheers when they saw the giant felled. Then they realized that Oisin was badly injured and exhausted. They took him gently between them and helped him back to the palace, where the queen put ointments and herbs on his wounds, and in a short time Oisin had recovered his health and spirits.

In the morning Niamh told Oisin that they must continue on their journey to Tir na n-Og. The sky darkened, the wind rose, and the boiling sea was lit by angry flashes. Niamh and Oisin rode steadily through the tempest, looking up at the pillars of cloud that glowed red, as lightning split the sky. As suddenly as it had begun, the storm abated, the fierce wind dropped, the waves calmed, and the sun shone brightly overhead.

There, amid the smooth, rich plains, a majestic castle glinted like a prism. Surrounding the castle were airy halls and summerhouses. As Niamh and Oisin approached the fortress, a troop of a hundred champions came out to meet them, their swords and shields shining in the sun.

Oisin was overwhelmed by the beauty of everything he saw. "Have we arrived at the Land of Youth?" he said at last.

"Indeed we have! This is Tir na n-Og," Niamh replied. "I told you the truth when I said how beautiful it was. And everything else I promised you, you will receive as well."

As Niamh spoke, a hundred beautiful young women came to meet them, dressed in silk and heavy brocade, and they welcomed the couple to Tir na n-Og. A huge, glittering crowd then approached and Oisin saw the king dressed in saffron silk, with a gold crown on his head, and beside him the queen, young and beautiful and attended by fifty girls who sang together as they crossed the green. When Niamh and Oisin met the royal party, the king took Oisin by the hand and welcomed him to his kingdom. Oisin thanked the king and queen, and a wedding feast was prepared for himself and Niamh. The festivities lasted for ten days and ten nights.

All that Niamh had promised came about, and Oisin lived happily in the Land of Youth with Niamh. Three children were born to them, and Niamh named one boy Finn in memory of Oisin's father and the other Oscar. Oisin gave his daughter a name that suited her loving nature and her lovely face; he named her Plur na mBan, the Flower of Women.

Three hundred years went by, though to Oisin they seemed as short as three. Then he began to get homesick for Ireland and lonely without the companionship of his friends, so he asked Niamh and her father to allow him to return home. The king consented, but Niamh begged him not to go.

Oisin tried to comfort his wife. "Don't be distressed, Niamh!" he said. "Our white horse knows the way. He'll bring me back safely."

So Niamh consented, but she gave Oisin a most solemn warning. "Listen to me, Oisin," she implored. "Do not dismount from the horse or you will never be able to return to this happy country. I say it again: If your foot as much as touches the ground while you are in Ireland, you will be lost forever to the Land of Youth!"

Then Niamh began to sob and wail. "Oisin, for the third time I warn you: Do not set foot on the soil of Ireland or you can never come back to me again. You should not go back, anyway! Everything is changed there. You will not see Finn or the Fianna. You will find only a crowd of monks and holy men."

Oisin consoled his wife as best he could, but Niamh pulled and clutched at her hair. His children were standing by, and as Oisin said farewell to them, his heart was heavy. As he stood by the white horse Niamh came up to him and kissed him. "Oh, Oisin," she sobbed, "here is a last kiss for you! You will never come back to me or the Land of Youth."

With a heavy heart Oisin mounted his horse and set out for Ireland. The horse took him away from Tir na n-Og as swiftly as it had brought Niamh and him there three hundred years before.

By the time Oisin arrived in Ireland, he was in high spirits, as strong and powerful a champion as he had ever been, and he set out at once to find the Fianna. He traveled over the familiar terrain where he had traveled so often with his companions, but saw no trace of any one of them. He went from one of Finn's haunts to another, but they were all deserted. He set out for the plains of Leinster and Almu, the place that he loved best. But when he arrived, there was no trace of the shining white fort. There was only a bare, windswept hill overgrown with ragwort, chickweed, and nettles. Oisin was heartbroken at the sight of the desolate place, and a tide of weariness washed over him as he realized that Finn and his companions were dead. With a heavy heart he left the Hill of Allen and headed eastward.

As he passed through Wicklow, through Glenasmole, the Valley of the Thrushes, he saw three hundred or more people crowding the glen. As Oisin approached, they stared at him curiously, astonished at his appearance and his great size. Then one of them shouted urgently, "Come over here and help us! You are much stronger than we are!" Oisin brought his horse closer to the crowd and saw that they were trying to lift up a vast marble flagstone. The stone was so great that the men underneath could not support it and were being crushed by the weight. Some were down already. Again the leader shouted desperately to Oisin, "Come quickly and help us lift the slab or all these men will be crushed to death!" Oisin looked down in disbelief at the crowd of men beneath him who were so puny and weak that they were unable to lift the flagstone. He leaned out of the saddle and, taking the marble slab in his hands, he raised it with all his strength and flung it away and the men underneath it were freed. But the slab was so heavy and the exertion so great that the golden girth round the horse's belly snapped, and Oisin was pulled sideways out of the saddle. He had to jump to the ground to save himself from falling, and the instant its rider's feet touched the ground, the horse bolted and galloped like the wind out of sight. Oisin stood upright for a moment, towering over the gathering. Then as the horrified crowd watched, the tall, young warrior, who had been stronger than all of them together, sank slowly to the ground. His powerful body withered and shrank, the skin on his handsome face wrinkled and sagged, and the sight left his clouded eyes. Hopeless and helpless, he lay at their feet, a bewildered, blind old man. But he lived to tell the tale, as did other tale-tellers after him. Patrick's scribes wrote these stories down and that is why Oisin and Finn, the Red Branch Heroes and the Tuatha De Danaan live on through their legends to this day.

PRONUNCIATION GUIDE

PRONUNCIATION OF IRISH NAMES AND WORDS

The following gives an approximate guide to the pronunciation of the Irish names and words that occur in the stories. Because there are both vowel and consonant sounds in the Irish language that do not exist in English, it is difficult to render the original sounds faithfully. What follows, therefore, is a simplified version of those sounds. The syllable that is stressed is in italics, and some words, whose pronunciation seems obvious, are included to indicate where the accent lies. Sometimes there is more than one way to pronounce the same word and I have given these alternatives where relevant.

   To make reading aloud easier, I have given separate pronunciation notes for each story. They are in order of appearance.

Sidhe   shee

MOYTURA
Moytura   moy-*toor*-a
Tuatha De Danaan   *too*-ha day *dan*-an
Fomorians   fo-*more*-ee-ans
Nuada   *noo*-a-ha
Balor   *bah*-lor
Eithlinn   *eth*-leen
Cian   *kee*-an
Birog   *birr*-ogue
Lugh   loo
Camall   *cam*-all
Ceithlinn   *keth*-leen
Morrigu (the)   *morr*-ig-oo

THE CHILDREN OF LIR
Fionnuala   finn-*noo*-la
Aed   ay (rhymes with day)
Fiacra   *fee*-ak-ra
Aoife   *eef*-eh
Bodb Dearg   bov *jar*-ag

Tuatha De Danaan   *too*-ha day *dan*-an
Derravaragh   der-ra-*va*-an
Carraignarone   carrig-na-*rone*
Mochaomhog   mo-*keev*-og
Lairgren   *lye*-er-gren

THE BIRTH OF CUCHULAINN
Cuchulainn   koo-*hull*-in / koo-*kull*-in
Conor Mac Nessa   *kon*-or mac *ness*-a
Emain Macha   *ev*-in *mach*-a / *ow*-in *mach*-a
   (ow rhymes with how)
Dechtire   *deck*-tir-a
Slieve Fuad   sleeve *foo*-ad
Bricriu   *brick*-roo
Lugh   loo
Finnchoem   *fin*-koo-em
Sencha   *shen*-ha
Morann   *mor*-an
Blai   *bla*-ee
Fergus   *fer*-gus
Amergin   *ah*-mer-gin / *ah*-ver-gin (hard g)
Dun Breth   doon breth

Sualdam Mac Roich   *soo*-al-dav mack *roy*
Setanta   shay-*tant*-a
Culann   *kull*-in
Cathbad   *kath*-vad / *kaff*-a

BRICRIU'S FEAST
Bricriu   *brick*-roo
Dun Rudraige   doon *ro*-ry
Emain Macha   *ev*-in *mach*-a / *ow*-in *mach*-a
   (ow rhymes with how)
Fergus   *fer*-gus
Laoghaire   *lair*-eh
Conall Cearnach   *kon*-all *kar*-nah
Cuchulainn   koo-*hull*-in / koo-*kull*-in
Sencha   *shen*-ha
Fidelma   fid-*dell*-ma
Lendabar   *len*-da-var
Emer   *ay*-ver / *ay*-mer
   (*ay* rhymes with day)
Cu Roi   koo *ree*

DEIRDRE OF THE SORROWS
Deirdre   *der*-dru
   (the u is barely sounded)
Felimid   *fell*-im-eed
Cathbad   *kath*-vad / *kaff*-a
Conor Mac Nessa   *kon*-or mac *ness*-a
Levercham   *lev*-er-ham
Naoise   *neesh*-eh
Usnach   *oosh*-na
Ardan   *aw*-ar-dawn
Ainnle   *awn*-leh
geis   gesh
Fergus   *fer*-gus
Dubhtach   *duv*-tah / *duff*-ach
Cormac   *kor*-moc
Emain Macha   *ev*-in *mach*-a / *ow*-in *mach*-a
   (ow rhymes with how)

Borrach   *bor*-ack
Fiacha   *fee*-ach-a
Eogan   *oh*-en (Owen)

THE SALMON OF KNOWLEDGE
Almu   *al*-moo
Tadg   *ta*-ig
Muirne   *mur*-na
Cumhaill   kool
Bascna   *bask*-na
Fianna   *fee*-a-na
Morna   *mor*-na
Cnuca   k-*nuck*-a
Demne   *dem*-na
Goll   gawl
Finn Mac Cumhaill   fin ma *kool*
Crimhall   *kriv*-al
Finnegas   fin-*ay*-gas (ay rhymes with day)

THE ENCHANTED DEER
Finn Mac Cumhaill   fin ma *kool*
Almu   *al*-moo
Sceolan   *skow*-lan
Sadb   sive (rhymes with dive)
Tuatha De Danaan   *too*-ha day *dan*-an
Fianna   *fee*-a-na
Lochlann   *loch*-lan
Oisin   ush-*een*

OISIN IN THE LAND OF YOUTH
Oisin   ush-*een*
Finn Mac Cumhaill   fin ma *kool*
Gowra   *gow*-ra (gow rhymes with how)
Niamh   *nee*-uv
Tir na n-Og   teer na nogue
Fomor   *foe*-more
Plur na mBan   *ploor* na *mawn*

SOURCE NOTES

I have listed below the main source or sources that I used for each story. I have added a further list of books which I found particularly helpful. Some of these are academic studies, and some are retellings. Incidents and details from a few of them have been incorporated here and there in my text.

THE MYTHOLOGICAL CYCLE

Moytura
Gray, Elizabeth A., *Cathe maig Tuired, The Second Battle of Mag Tuired*, Irish Texts Society, Dublin, 1982

Gregory, Augusta, *Gods and Fighting Men*, London, 1904

The Children of Lir
O'Curry, Eugene, "The Three Most Sorrowful Tales of Erinn," from *Atlantis* IV, Dublin, 1858

THE ULSTER CYCLE

The Birth of Cuchulainn
Hull, Eleanor (ed.), *The Cúchullin Saga in Irish Literature*, London, 1898

Bricriu's Feast
Cross, Tom Peete and Slover, Clark H., *Ancient Irish Tales*, London, 1937

Deirdre of the Sorrows
O'Flanagan, Theophilus, "Deirdri," *Transactions of the Gaelic Society of Dublin*, 1808

THE FINN CYCLE

Finn and the Salmon of Knowledge
Hennessy, W.M., *Revenue Celtique* II, Paris, 1873–5

Kennedy, Patrick, *Legendary Fictions of the Irish Celts*, London 1891

O'Donovan, John, "The Boyish Exploits of Finn Mac Cumhill" from *Transactions of the Ossianic Society* IV, Dublin, 1859

O'Grady, Standish Hayes, *Silva Gadelica*, Dublin, 1892

Mac Neill, Eoin, *Duanaire Finn* I, Irish Texts Society, London, 1908

The Enchanted Deer
Kennedy, Patrick, *Legendary Fictions of the Irish Celts*, London, 1891

Oisin in the Land of Youth
O'Looney, B., *Transactions of the Ossianic Society* IV, Dublin, 1859

Joyce, P.W., *Old Celtic Romances*, London, 1914

Cross, Tom Peete and Slover, Clark H., *Ancient Irish Tales*, London, 1937

Campbell, J.J., *Legends of Ireland*, London, 1955

FURTHER READING

Coghlan, Ronan, *Pocket Dictionary of Irish Myth and Legend*, Belfast, 1985

Curtain, Jeremiah, *Hero Tales of Ireland*, Dublin, 1894

Dillon, Myles *The Cycle of the Kings*, London, 1947

—*Early Irish Literature*, Chicago, 1948

—*Irish Sagas*, Dublin, 1954

Ellis, P. Berresford, *A Dictionary of Irish Mythology*, London, 1987

Flower, Robin, *The Irish Tradition*, Oxford, 1947

Green, Miranda J., *A Dictionary of Celtic Myth and Legend*, London, 1992

Gregory, Augustus, *The Blessed Trinity of Ireland*, London, 1985

Hull, Eleanor, *Cuchulain—the Hound of Ulster*, London, 1909

Hyde, Douglas, *The Three Sorrows of Storytelling*, London, 1895

Jackson, Kenneth Hurlstone, *A Celtic Miscellany*, London, 1951

Kavanagh, Peter, *Irish Mythology*, New York, 1959

Kinsella, Thomas, *The Tain*, Oxford, 1970

Kinsella, Thomas (ed.), *The New Oxford Book of Irish Verse*, Oxford, 1986

Mac Cana, Proinsias, *Celtic Mythology*, London, 1970

Mac Neill, Eoin, *Duanaire Finn* I, London, 1908

Meyer, Kuno, *Death Tales of the Ulster Heroes*, Dublin, 1913

—and Nutt, Alfred, *The Voyage of Bran, Son of Febal*, London, 1895

Montague, John (ed.), *The Faber Book of Irish Verse*, London, 1974

Murphy, Gerard, *Duanaire Finn* II, London, 1933

Nutt, Alfred, *Ossian and Ossianic Literature*, London, 1899

—*Cúchulainn: The Irish Achilles*, London, 1900

O'Connor, Frank, *Kings, Lords and Commons: An Anthology from the Irish*, New York, 1959

—*The Little Monasteries*, Dublin, 1963

O'Faolain, Eileen, *Irish Sagas and Folk Tales*, London, 1954

O'Grady, Standish Hayes, *Silva Gadelica*, 2 vols, Dublin, 1893

O'Grady, Standish James, *Fionn and His Companions*, Dublin, 1892

—*The Coming of Cuchulain*, London, 1894

—*The Triumph and Passing of Cuchulain*, London, 1920

O'Hogain, Daithi, *Myth, Legend and Romance*, London, 1990

O'Rahilly, Cecile, *Táin Bó Cuailgne* (from the Book of Leinster), Dublin, 1967

—*Táin Bó Cuailgne* (from the Book of the Dun Cow), Dublin, 1978

O'Rahilly, Thomas F., *Early Irish History and Mythology*, Dublin 1946

Rees, Alwyn and Brinley, *Celtic Heritage*, London, 1961

Rolleston, T.W., *Myths and Legends of the Celtic Race*, London, 1912

—*The High Deeds of Fionn*, London, 1910

Smyth, Daragh, *A Guide to Irish Mythology*, Dublin, 1988

Sjoestedt, M.L., *Gods and Heroes of the Celts*, Paris, 1949

Stephens, James, *Irish Fairy Tales*, London, 1924

MARIE HEANEY was born in County Tyrone, Ireland. She was trained as a teacher in Northern Ireland and received a master's degree in Irish Studies at University College, Dublin. She writes for both television and newspapers, and recently published a collection for adults, *Over Nine Waves: A Book of Irish Legend*. She says of the stories in *The Names Upon the Harp*: "What ensures their place in world literature is their agelessness, their value as expressions of the perennial art of the storyteller." Ms. Heaney lives in Dublin with her husband, poet Seamus Heaney, and their three children.

P. J. LYNCH has been honored with many awards and citations for his illustrations, including the prestigious Kate Greenaway Medal, which he won twice, first for *The Christmas Miracle of Jonathan Toomey*, by Susan Wojciechowski, and then for *When Jessie Came Across the Sea*, by Amy Hest.

Since childhood he has had images of Finn, the son of Cumhaill, and leader of the Fianna; Conor Mac Nessa, King of Ulster; and, Cuchulainn, the great hero, in his head. But only in collaboration with a storyteller as respected as Marie Heaney did he feel ready to commit those images to paper. Mr. Lynch makes his home in Dublin, Ireland.

So You Have to Do a Science Fair Project

Joyce Henderson
Heather Tomasello

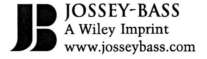

JOSSEY-BASS
A Wiley Imprint
www.josseybass.com

Published by Jossey-Bass
A Wiley Imprint
989 Market Street, San Francisco, CA 94103-1741   www.josseybass.com

Published simultaneously in Canada

Design and production by Navta Associates, Inc.

Jossey-Bass books and products are available through most bookstores. To contact Jossey-Bass directly call our Customer Care Department within the U.S. at 800-956-7739, outside the U.S. at 317-572-3986, or fax 317-572-4002.

Jossey-Bass also publishes its books in a variety of electronic formats. Some content that appears in print may not be available in electronic books.

ISBN 0-471-20256-8

FIRST EDITION
PB Printing   10 9 8 7 6 5 4 3 2

To
Dr. John Cech, teacher, mentor, and friend
and
Colby Stephen, born the day after the book was finished

Contents

 So You Have to Do a Science Fair Project   1

Begin with a Question   2

Get out Your Logbook   6

Who Cares?   6

 Where Do You Begin?: Project Ideas   9

Biological Projects   10

Physical Projects   13

Environmental Projects   15

 **Gathering Information: Think of It as
a Treasure Hunt   17**

What Do You Already Know and What Do
    You Need to Find Out?   20

Where Should You Look for Information?   20

Think of Key Words   20

Using the Internet   20

Ask an Expert   23

Organizing Your Information   24

Write Down the Source of Each Piece of
    Information   26

Guess What? The Hypothesis   29

The Null Hypothesis   32

Prove It or Not   32

Test Your Guess: Experimentation   33

A Recipe for Success: The Procedure   34

Controls and Variables   36

Safety   39

Materials   39

Just Do It!   41

What If You Encounter Trouble?   42

Write It Down: Recording Your Observations   45

Tables   47

A Picture Is Worth a Thousand Words   51

Get It All Together: Organizing Your Data   53

Showing Qualitative Results   54

Showing Quantitative Results   54

What Is an Average?   55

Bar Graphs   56

Line Graphs   57

Pie Charts   59

Pick up the Pieces: The Research Paper   63

Title, Hypothesis, and Purpose   66

Background   67

Materials List and Procedure   67

Results   68

Conclusions   69

The Bibliography   69

Finishing Touches   69

How Long Should the Paper Be?   72

The Abstract   73

9 Show It Off: The Backboard   75

The Display   77

What Is a Backboard?   77

Cardboard Backboards   77

Building Your Own Backboard   78

Backboard Blues   80

All That Space   80

Putting It All Together   81

Mounting Mats and Papers   83

What Goes Where   84

Titles   85

Get Creative!   86

10 Make It Perfect: Finishing Touches   87

Table and Cloth   88

Photographs   88

Drawings   89

Your Research Paper   89

Reprints File   90

Resource Books   90

Your Logbook   90

Computers   90

Models   91

Effective Displays   92

11 Give It Your All: The Science Fair   95

Dress to Impress   96

Know What to Say   97

All Done?   100

What If the Judge Asks Me Something I Don't
    Know?   100

What Do Judges Want to See?   101

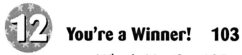 **You're a Winner! 103**

What's Next? 105

Beyond Your Local Science Fair 105

Glossary 113

Index 115

1 So You Have to Do a Science Fair Project

So, you have to do a science fair project. Maybe you really want to. Maybe your parents want you to. Maybe your teacher is making you.

And you're probably thinking: this is going to be hard! Science fair projects involve a lot of work.

They're also a lot of fun. And the work isn't so hard when you break it into steps and take it one step at a time.

This book is for kids who want to do their own project but need a little help along the way. It is also for parents who never had to do a science fair project and don't have a clue where to start when their child comes home and says, "I have to do a project."

Why would you *want* to do a science fair project? Because it is fun! You can pick a topic that is interesting to you. You can answer a question you might have wondered about. You can do something different from everyone else in your class.

Begin with a Question

First you need to choose a topic or a question for your project. You'll answer the question in your experiment. The best project is one that interests you.

Your Road Map
The Scientific Method

Doing a science fair project is like taking a long trip some place you've never been before. What would you usually take with you on a trip to a new place? Directions, right?

The **scientific method** will provide your directions for the journey that is your project. Here are the five basic steps in the scientific method:

Step 1: Select a topic or a question.

Step 2: Gather information about the topic. What do you need to know to answer the question?

Step 3: What do you think the answer to your question will be? This guess is known as your hypothesis.

Step 4: Test your guess through experimentation.

Step 5: Make conclusions based on the results of that testing.

Random Acts of Attitude

The secret to your child's science fair success begins with your attitude. Attitudes are contagious, and you want yours to be worth catching! When your child brings home his science fair assignment, your reaction may be somewhere between a wildly excited ninth-grade cheerleader and a desperate drowning victim. Try to strike a balance between these two extremes. What your child needs is for you to be encouraging and enthusiastic.

This book will help you get through every step without ever having to put the tip of a marking pen to the poster board of a display. Each chapter contains "Just for Parents": tips and advice for you as the mom or dad of a science fair student.

This book is designed to be a guide for students between first and sixth grades. Your child can do all of the work himself, and along the way he'll learn more about creativity, cause-and-effect relationships, logical reasoning, problem-solving, writing, and speaking skills. Your child's project will be his own, and you can both be proud of his efforts. We don't guarantee he'll win any awards, but he'll be a winner!

Usually, the first or second science fair experience is a teacher-assigned mandatory project, but as your student gets into the middle high and senior high years, science fair participation is often elective. These are the years when he'll gain valuable skills and have the opportunity to compete for awards and scholarships. If your child shows interest and aptitude in the elementary years, encourage him to stick with science fairs. It will be well worth the effort in the coming years!

You probably think of dozens of these kinds of questions every day without realizing it. Questions like:

- Will milk spoil faster if it is left out of the refrigerator?
- Which battery lasts longer?
- How does acid rain affect plants?
- Does the largest popcorn kernel produce the largest piece of popped popcorn?

Sometimes it helps to think about types of projects that might interest you. Most fairs have three main categories: *physical, biological,* and *environmental.*

- *Physical* sciences include the study of planets and stars, rocks, weather, math, how things work, and chemistry.
- *Biological* projects have to do with living things, such as plants, bugs, germs, animals, and people.
- *Environmental* projects ask questions about the changes in the world around you. What affects the air you breathe and the water you drink? How are things recycled? How does pollution affect plants?

Just for practice, write down four or five questions of your own. They can be about anything you happen to think of. Don't worry for now about whether or not they would make good science fair projects.

Many of the projects in this book can be modified to suit your interests or the materials that are available to you. For example, what if you decide to study the question "Which color attracts a bee?" You might choose three different-colored flowers of the same kind and observe which one attracts the most bees. If you don't have access to bees but there are hummingbirds in your backyard, you might study which color of feeding station attracts the most hummingbirds. Or you might try hanging different-colored pieces of wood in an area where there are spider webs to see which one attracts the most spider webs.

● *interesting to you.* This is the most important part. Choose something you enjoy! It will be hard work and *no* fun if you don't like your topic or are bored with it.

● *one that you can do in the amount of time you have before the science fair.* Maybe you have three months, maybe you have three weeks. (And we sure hope you're not starting the night before the fair!) You need a project you can do in the time you have. This will involve doing research, performing an experiment, writing a report, and making a poster or display.

● *something you can do by yourself (or with a little help).* This is your project. Your parents and teacher can help you, but they can't do it for you.

● *one that's really possible for you to do.* Sometimes a project looks really interesting, but you can't do it because you're allergic to hamsters, or you can't build a space shuttle in your backyard.

● *one that includes an experiment and is more than just a report.* You must test a question, not just build a model or write a report.

● *safe!* Some projects are too dangerous for you to do. Science fair rules prohibit experiments that use certain chemicals or bacteria. Check with your teacher or local science fair organizer for specific rules. And no project should harm animals or little brothers!

A project on the behavior of mice might also work for gerbils, hamsters, or other similar animals. Think about what you could change to make your project better fit your interests, abilities, or available materials.

Get out Your Logbook

This is a good time to begin a **logbook.** It doesn't have to be anything fancy—a simple spiral-bound notebook or a composition-type notebook will do. Use the logbook to record each step of doing your project. Even if your teacher doesn't require you to keep a logbook, we recommend it. It's a good way to keep track of everything you need to know and do for your project. Don't worry about neatness either. The logbook is not your final report.

After you've decided on an idea, discuss it with your teacher and a parent. Once they have approved it, you can begin the next step—researching. If you've already chosen your project topic, you can skip ahead to Chapter 3. But if you're still stuck for an idea, look through the project topics in Chapter 2.

BRAINSTORM!

In your logbook write down a project question you've thought of, or choose one from the list in the next chapter. Why did you choose this question? Look at your question and compare it to each of the items in "The Best Project Is . . ." list. Can you answer yes to all the points? If not, try another question or project and compare it to the list.

Who Cares?

Your project needs to have a **purpose.** Think about why you want to do this project. Is there a reason this project is important? Will the results help someone have a better life? Will what you learn be helpful to you? Is there a problem that you can solve?

These questions refer to what in later years will be known as a "practical application"—or the "who cares" factor.

Whose Project Is This Anyway?

The science fair is a wonderful opportunity for learning. A project brings together every skill a student needs to be successful throughout her school career. Your child will learn how to choose a topic, research it, conduct an experiment, record the results, and share those results. She will need to use almost every subject she studies: English, spelling, reading, grammar, math, and science.

This is the time, before any work has even begun, to erase a single phrase from your vocabulary: "We'll do it together." Kids who don't want to be seen with their parents in the mall definitely don't want to go to the library with them.

Instead, agree with your child that this is her project. You can help in several ways, but your child is responsible for the whole thing.

Your child's first step in doing a project involves selecting a topic. This is an important first step. Forget the projects you did in school or the ten ideas you immediately have for perfectly wonderful science fair projects. Let your child choose her own topic. Give guidance in the form of suggesting topics that conform to her interests or natural abilities, but don't get carried away and describe how she should do the project.

Narrow the search first to a category, then present two or three ideas within that category. After your child chooses a topic, be sure to check with the teacher for approval before encouraging your child to take the next step. The teacher may suggest ways to refine the project or different directions in which to take it.

Why is your project important? Anyone can do a little research, conduct an experiment, and get results. But at the heart of the scientific method is *problem-solving*. Ribbons are not awarded because your poster board looks colorful or you had a neat idea. Science fair winners choose a project that solves a problem.

Write down the answers to these questions in your logbook:

1. Why is my project important?

2. What problem might I solve?

3. What will I learn from doing this project?

2 Where Do You Begin?

Project Ideas

How to Help Your Child Use This List

We offer these suggestions not so that your son or daughter can do a project that's already been done, but in the hopes that one of them will spark an idea for your child.

Several of the ideas listed here involve brand comparison, such as, "Which kind of soda do students prefer?" or, "Which detergent works best?" These projects are probably not appropriate for the older student. However, for a child who is younger or doing a first project, they can be valuable for several reasons. Brand comparisons involve materials that are easy to get. These projects can usually be done at home and do not require weeks of experimentation. The most important aspects of a science fair project for the young child are experiencing the scientific method in action and having his natural curiosity sparked. The brand comparison project accomplishes these goals and is a stepping-stone to more sophisticated projects.

The experiments listed here are divided according to grade-appropriate levels. The lists are designed to be flexible, however. A very advanced third-grader might choose a project listed under Grades 4–6. Also, because each student approaches a question differently, the variations for these projects are endless. Even the most basic-looking topic can yield an award-winning project and a great learning experience!

re you still stumped for a project idea? This chapter has plenty of ideas for you to consider. As you think about possibilities for your science fair project, remember to pick a question that interests you! After all, you're going to have to research the subject, write a paper, and design an experiment. A science fair project involves more than just building a model or making a drawing to show something. So choose a topic that will be fun and that you think will make a good experiment.

Biological Projects

Grades 1–3

Projects about plants

- How does fertilizer affect plants' rates of growth?
- How does light affect the ripening of fruit?
- How does heat affect the ripening of fruit?
- Does the depth of planting affect the height of a seedling?
- Will seedlings planted upside down grow upside down?
- Do plants grow toward sunlight?

Projects about animals

- Which foods do cats (dogs, fishes, etc.) prefer?
- Do birds prefer popped or unpopped corn?
- Can a mouse (gerbil, hamster) learn to run a maze?
- Which color of fishing lure catches the most fish?
- Which foods attract/repel insects?

Projects about people

- Are boys my age taller than girls my age?
- Do kids my age prefer one soft drink over another?
- Which brand of fast-food french fries do kids my age like best?
- Are left thumbprints identical to right thumbprints?

Read through the list and write down any questions that interest you. Then discuss those ideas with your teacher or parent.

Miscellaneous

- Does temperature affect odor?
- Is soil a better insulator than air?

Grades 4–6

Projects about plants

- How do plants get nitrogen?
- How does water move through a plant?
- How do changes in the length of the day affect plant growth?
- What is the effect of organic matter on the growth of plants?
- What is the effect of temperature on the germination of seeds?
- What is the effect of microwave radiation on the germination of seeds?
- Does presoaking seeds affect the germination and growth of plants?
- What is the effect of electric current on plants?
- What is the effect of secondhand smoke on plants?
- Do vegetables grown in lead-contaminated soil contain lead?

Projects about animals

- Do hamsters (mice, gerbils) need vitamins?
- Under what conditions do butterflies hatch faster?
- How do earthworms affect the soil they live in?
- Can flatworms (planaria) regrow heads or tails?
- Whose mouth has the most bacteria, humans' or dogs'?
- Which soap kills the most germs?
- Which kind of bread grows the most mold, white or wheat?
- Can bacteria be found in canned baby formula?
- Can lysozyme kill bacteria?
- Do marine sponges kill bacteria?

Projects about people

- Who remembers dreams more often, boys or girls?
- Do girls or boys my age have better short-term memory?
- How does listening to different kinds of music affect a person's heart rate?
- Do babies prefer certain colors?

- Do certain colors affect people's moods?
- What are the effects of video games on a person's heart rate?
- How does music affect short-term memory?
- How does left-brain dominance compare to right-brain dominance in people?
- Is brain dominance inherited?
- How does eating different sweeteners affect a person's weight?

Miscellaneous
- How does a tooth decay?
- How safe are soda cans?
- Are homes cleaner eating places than public places?

Physical Projects

Grades 1–3

Projects about electricity
- Which metals conduct electricity (heat) best?
- How can heat produce electricity?
- Which battery lasts longest?
- How do waves carry energy?
- How does the amount of oxygen affect the rate of burning?
- What products result from burning a candle?
- Do fluorescent lights last longer than filament bulbs?

Projects about geology
- How are rocks classified?
- What factors affect the growth of crystals?

Projects about chemistry
- Which brand of orange juice has the highest vitamin C content?
- Which detergent (toothpaste, deodorant, shampoo) works best?
- Which gum blows the biggest bubbles?
- Which metal rusts faster?

Miscellaneous
- How does surface area affect evaporation time?

- Do some numbers come up in the lottery more frequently than others?
- Is a black shirt hotter than a white one on a sunny day?

Grades 4–6

Projects about electricity

- How is electrical current affected by the type of conductor (temperature, filament)?
- Can a potato generate electricity?

Projects about chemistry

- What is the effect of salt on the freezing point of water and other liquids?
- What happens to the volume of water when it freezes?
- Does temperature affect solubility?
- Are some substances more soluble than others?
- What is the effect of temperature on the solubility of a gas in a liquid?
- How is light affected by passing through water?
- Which gas is most dense?
- What gas is produced when seltzer reacts with water?
- Can I blow square bubbles?
- What is an anti-bubble?
- How can the oxidation of fruits be prevented?
- What is the tensile strength of fibers exposed to water (salt, bleach, soil, flames)?

Miscellaneous

- Can the thickness of ice at the center of a lake be determined by measuring the ice at the shore?
- What is the effect of inflation pressure on the distance a soccer ball can be kicked?
- Which rocket fin design is the most aerodynamically stable?
- Does wing shape affect velocity?
- What is the best wing shape for an airplane?
- What limits the speed of a boat (truck)?
- How accurate are homemade weather-detecting instruments?
- How does baseball filler (cork, sawdust, rubber) affect the distance a ball travels?

- Can I hit a baseball with an aluminum bat better than with a wooden one?
- What kinds of structures hold the most weight?
- Which magnet is the strongest?
- How do metals compare in density and buoyancy?
- How does gravity affect weight?
- Can a model train be run by a computer?
- What is the relationship between the size of kernels and the size of popped popcorn?
- How does temperature affect the rate of popcorn popping?
- Which method pops popcorn faster, air or oil?

Environmental Projects

Grades 1–3

Projects about plants

- How can I grow plants hydroponically?
- How can soil erosion be prevented?
- How is water passing through the ground naturally filtered?
- How does composting help the garden?

Projects about pollution

- What causes air (water) pollution?
- How does air pollution (carbon dioxide) affect plants?
- How can air pollution be cleaned up?
- How does acid rain affect the acidity of soil?

Miscellaneous

- How can solar energy be used to heat a room?
- Is there a relationship between temperature and humidity?
- How can heat be spread more evenly throughout a house?
- What is the best insulation for homes?

Grades 4–6

Projects about plants

- How can pests be controlled naturally?

- What can be learned from tree rings?
- Do vegetables grown using pesticides differ in flavor from those grown organically?
- Which fruits (vegetables) produce the best natural dyes?
- Does noise pollution affect the growth of plants?
- How does acid rain affect plants?
- How does overcrowding affect plant growth?
- How are lichens (mosses, ferns) affected by acid rain?
- Do some plants absorb more carbon dioxide than others?
- Are some plants more resistant to air pollution than others?

Projects about pollution

- Paper or plastic bags—which is better for the environment?
- Under which conditions will plastic bags biodegrade best?
- How much trash does the average household in my community create per week? How can this amount be reduced?
- What percentage of the families in my community participate in municipal recycling programs? How does this compare to the national average?
- What is the most common roadside litter in my community?
- Which commercial water purifier works best?
- Can acid rain be detected in my community? If so, what can be done about it?
- How does acid rain affect buildings (statues)?
- Can fertilizer runoff be found in my community's river? If so, what can be done about it?
- How can a pollutant such as phosphate be removed from water?
- What is the best way to soak up oil from oil spills?

Miscellaneous

- Can salt be removed from seawater by freezing the water?
- What introduced species of plants (or animals) can be found in my community? How do they impact its native species?
- Does noise pollution affect mental concentration?
- Is it more cost-efficient to recycle glass, aluminum, paper, or plastic?
- What does the greenhouse effect do to the surface temperature of the earth?

3 Gathering Information

Think of It as a Treasure Hunt

ow that you've selected a topic or question for your project, you're off on the hunt for information. Like a pirate searching for buried treasure, you must find everything you need to know in order to plan your experiment. It helps a lot to know *what* you're looking for and *where* to look. Be warned, however, that researching your project can take more time than doing the actual experiment, so allow yourself plenty of time for this part of your journey!

BRAINSTORM!

irst, figure out what you already know about your project and write that down in a column in your logbook. Then think about what you might need to learn in order to answer your experimental question. Write these questions in another column in your logbook. Take a look at the samples provided here.

(Grades 1–3)

Sample Project #1

"Will Milk Spoil Faster If Left out of the Refrigerator?"

What Do I Already Know About My Question?

1. Milk spoils.
2. We store milk in a refrigerator.
3. Milk comes from cows.
4. Milk cartons have a freshness date on them.

What Else Do I Need to Know?

1. How can I tell when milk has spoiled?
2. What is the temperature inside our refrigerator and outside the refrigerator in the kitchen?
3. What happens to milk after it is taken from the cow? Is anything done to it to make it last longer?
4. Who gives milk its freshness date? Why? What does the date mean?

Sample Project #2

"Which Battery Lasts Longest?"

What Do I Already Know About My Question?

1. There are several different brands of batteries.
2. One brand makes the claim that it lasts longest.
3. My flashlight uses batteries.

What Else Do I Need to Know?

1. How does a battery work?
2. Do different brands work differently?
3. Can I use a flashlight to test different batteries to see which lasts longer?

Sample Project #3

"How Does Acid Rain Affect Plants?"

What Do I Already Know About My Question?

1. Plants need rain or water to live.
2. I've heard that acid rain is bad for plants.

What Else Do I Need to Know?

1. What is acid rain?
2. What causes acid rain?
3. How does acid rain affect plants?

Sample Project #4

"Does the Largest Popcorn Kernel Produce the Largest Piece of Popped Popcorn?"?"

What Do I Already Know About My Question?

1. Popped popcorn comes from kernels.
2. Popcorn comes in different varieties and colors.

What Else Do I Need to Know?

1. Do different colors or varieties of popcorn produce larger popped popcorn?
2. Does the size of the unpopped kernel affect the size of the popped piece?

What Do You Already Know and What Do You Need to Find Out?

You can wander for hours in the library or on the Internet. There is so much information out there on anything and everything you ever wanted to know! To avoid getting lost, you need to be organized in your search for information.

Where Should You Look for Information?

Take your notebook or logbook with your questions, along with pencils and a pack of index cards, and head to the library! The reference librarian can show you how to use the computers or the card file to find information about your project. "References" are the books, magazine articles, and encyclopedias that you use to look up information. Look at all of these kinds of **sources.** (A source is a place where you find information.) You may find the same information in more than one source. That is okay because you need more than one book or article as a source of information for your project.

You may check out most of the books and take them home to study them. Magazine articles and information in reference books, such as encyclopedias, usually can't be taken out of the library. Instead, you'll need to take notes at the library on those index cards. Or you might photocopy any pages you want to keep for future reference. Be sure to take plenty of change with you for the copy machine.

Think of Key Words

The easiest way to search is to identify **key words** about your project. Then search for books, newspaper or magazine articles, and encyclopedia entries that contain those key words.

What might be some key words for the sample projects in this chapter?

Using the Internet

If you have a computer and access to the Internet at home, at school, or at the local library, you may use it to do some, but definitely not all, of your research. Be aware first that the Internet is *not* a giant library and that the information you find on it may not be correct. The Internet is a great place to find an idea for a project and get some

Sample Key Words

Project Question	Possible Key Words
Will milk spoil faster if left out of the refrigerator?	Milk Dairy cow Spoiling Refrigeration Expiration date
Which battery lasts longest?	Battery Electricity Volts
How does acid rain affect plants?	Acid rain Pollution Watering plants
Does the largest popcorn kernel produce the largest piece of popped popcorn?	Popcorn Kernel

general background on your idea. The Internet should *never* be your only source of information about your project. The Internet can also be a time-waster because it is so easy to get distracted by too much information and wander away from the path of your project.

If you've never done an Internet search, ask a parent or teacher or librarian for help. You first need to open a search engine such as Yahoo.com or Google.com. From there, you just have to type in a key word or words in the box provided and click on "search." You'll most likely need to narrow the search by using several key words instead of just one.

BRAINSTORM!

Write down your own list of key words in your logbook before you go to the library. Don't worry if the list seems short. As you begin to look for information, you may find other key words. Keep your list handy, and add the new key words to it.

PARENTS

Wandering the Internet

Never allow your child to wander the Internet alone. Whether in the library or at home, stay with your child when he uses the Internet. The best way you can help is to keep him from becoming sidetracked as he pursues every little bit of information available at his fingertips. The use of computers also tempts students to cut and paste information directly from the source. Explain to your child that this is plagiarism, and always encourage your child to write what he learns in his own words.

Ask an Expert

Many times you will be able to find an expert who can give you information about your subject. Do the same type of "key word" search in the yellow pages of the telephone book. Ask your teacher or parents if they know anyone who might answer some questions about your project. Check at a local university or hospital.

Write down questions first before you talk to an expert. You can't simply call and say, "Tell me all that you know about bacteria or guinea pigs." Most people are eager to share information with you, but they need to know exactly what information you want.

Ask the expert if it is easier for him to answer your questions in writing or in person. If he is a very busy person, he may wish to receive a list of written questions and answer them when he has time. Or he may want you to visit his place of work and see firsthand whatever he can show you. Keep in mind that these people are busy and may have only a few minutes to take from their jobs to share with you.

Where to Look for Local Experts

1. *A nursery, florist, or farmer:* for projects about or using plants

2. *A veterinarian or pet store:* for projects about or using animals

3. *A hospital laboratory or doctor:* for projects involving bacteria, health, or using sterile technique

4. *An engineer:* for projects involving structures or building models

5. *A pharmacist:* for information about how drugs or vitamins work

6. *A computer repair person or computer engineer:* for information about computers

7. *A psychiatrist or psychologist:* for projects about behavior or brain dominance

8. *A naturalist, environmental educator, or park ranger:* for projects about the environment, plants, or pollution

The Best Sources of Information Are . . .

1. *. . . up-to-date.* Check the date in the front of the book or magazine. What we knew about many areas of science twenty or thirty years ago is very different from what we know today.

2. *. . . not all the same.* You should use different kinds of sources, such as books, magazines, encyclopedias, the Internet, and personal interviews.

3. *. . . easy to understand.* If there's something in an information source you don't understand, ask your teacher or parents for help.

Write down the information from an interview on index cards just as you would with any other source. Write the name of the expert and the date and time of the interview on the back of the card. It is helpful to ask the expert to give you a business card. That way you'll have his name, address, and telephone number. Be sure you write a thank-you note whenever anyone helps you.

Asking an expert is only one way to obtain information about your topic. You still need to find more information by researching other sources. Be sure to ask an expert whether he can suggest other sources of information.

Organizing Your Information

The easiest way to organize the information you find during your research is using index cards. These can be three-by-five-inch cards, or four-by-six-inch if the larger size is more convenient for you. For each key word, you should have at least one card. You may have more than one. When you find the information in a book or article, write on the index card what you read, but be sure you write the information in your own words. Here's what several cards from one of the sample projects might look like:

Key Word: Acid Rain

What is acid rain? Happens when fossil fuels like coal, oil, natural gas are burned and pollution goes into the atmosphere.

[on the back of the card]

Source: Miller, Christina. _Acid Rain: A Sourcebook for Young People._ Simon & Schuster: NY, 1986. pp. 5–6.

Key Word: Air Pollution

Common kinds of pollution: sulfur dioxide and nitrogen oxides. These + water + sunlight = sulfuric and nitric acid. When it rains (or snows, etc.) they fall to the ground.

[on the back of the card]

Source: Miller, Christina. _Acid Rain: A Sourcebook for Young People._ Simon & Schuster: NY, 1986. p. 6.

Key Word: Effects on Plants

These acids can harm plants. They get into the leaves through small holes (pores). "In U.S., pollution destroys $2-5 billion in crops each year and reduces food production by 5-10%."

[on the back of the card]

Source: Kahl, Jonathan. <u>Hazy Skies:</u> <u>Weather and the Environment.</u> Lerner Publications: MN, 1998. p. 28.

When you are working with copies of articles or printouts of information from a computer source, you may want to highlight the information with a colored marker so that you can easily find it again. But you should still write the information in your own words on an index card.

Index cards are better than the pages of a notebook because they can be sorted according to subject (key words). With all of them laid out in front of you while you are working on your paper, you won't miss any crucial facts.

Write Down the Source of Each Piece of Information

The source where you find information is very important. Knowing where the information comes from tells your teacher that you did your research, and that the information is reliable. Also, if you ever need to go back and look up something again, it is much easier if you have kept track of where the information comes from.

On the back of each index card, write down the name of the author of the book (last name first), the title of the book (underline this), the name of the publisher, and where and when it was published. You'll find all of that on the first and second pages of the book. If the book has been printed several times, use the most recent date. If your teacher asks for a **bibliography** or **citation** in your report, this is the information you'll use. Here are the formats to use, depending on the type of source:

Sample Citations

Book Citation

Author's last name, first name. Title of book *(underlined)*. Publisher's name: place, year.

Example: Berger, Gilda. <u>Sharks</u>. Doubleday: NY, 1987.

Magazine Citation

Author's last name, first name. Title of article *(quotation marks before and after)*. Name of the magazine *(underlined)*. Date of publication, volume number, page number(s).

Example: Zao, Richard. "Global Warming: The Latest Trends." <u>Time Magazine.</u> October 2000, 12, 57–59.

Internet Citation

Author's last name, first name. Title of article or web site, web site address. Date accessed.

Example: Lyman, Isabel. "What's Behind the Growth in Homeschooling," www.findarticles.com. Accessed August 8, 2001.

Encyclopedia Citation

There probably won't be an author's name, so just begin with the name of the book. Then follow the citation for a book.

Example: Webster's New World Encyclopedia. Prentice-Hall: NY, 1993.

Expert Interview Citation

When you ask an expert for information, write the name of the expert *(last name first)*, the words "Personal interview," and the date.

Example: Nobles, Shawn. Personal interview. December 12, 2001.

If there is more than one date of publication, use the most recent one. If there are two authors, list both names. For more than two authors, you only have to write the first one's name, followed by the words "et al.," which mean "and all."

Citations are just as important as finding and using the information, so be sure you pay attention to keeping track of the sources you use. You'll need that information later when you write your research paper.

4 Guess What?

The Hypothesis

The next step on your journey is to make a guess at what will happen when you do the experiment for your project. You may have an idea of what the results will be. What you think will happen is called the **hypothesis.** Some students call this the "hypo-the-guess."

You probably already enjoy asking questions and looking for answers. The process of searching for information, making a hypothesis, and testing that hypothesis turns ordinary curiosity into a science project.

It may feel awkward at first guessing about the outcome of the experiment before you even do it, but you'll be surprised at how easy this step really is. Since you've already done the **background** research, your hypothesis will actually be an educated guess!

Let's look at some examples. If you were testing the question "How does acid rain affect plants?" you probably have a guess about what will happen. Your hypothesis could be: "Plants exposed to acid rain take longer to grow."

Many science fair projects are investigations of cause-and-effect relationships. For example, consider the project "Will Acid Rain Affect

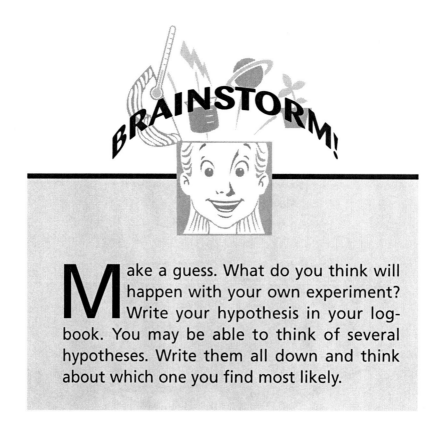

Make a guess. What do you think will happen with your own experiment? Write your hypothesis in your logbook. You may be able to think of several hypotheses. Write them all down and think about which one you find most likely.

a Plant's Growth?" The cause is acid rain. From your research, you may expect a certain effect: acid rain will cause plants to grow more slowly.

Other projects compare one thing to several others. The project "Which Battery Lasts Longest?" compares the lasting power of several different batteries. From your research, you know that some batteries are more expensive than others and make claims that they last longer. You may guess that the most expensive battery of the ones you're testing will last longer than the others. Call it "Battery A." So your hypothesis is: Battery A will last longer than Batteries B, C, and D.

Let's look at some other projects. What might the hypothesis for each of them be?

Sample Hypotheses

Project Question	Possible Hypothesis
1. Does the largest popcorn kernel produce the largest piece of popped popcorn?	**1.** The largest popcorn kernel will produce the largest piece of popped popcorn.
2. Can a gerbil be taught to run a maze?	**2.** A gerbil can be taught to run a maze.
3. Which color attracts hummingbirds?	**3.** A red feeder will attract more hummingbirds than a white, blue, or green feeder.
4. Is a black shirt hotter than a white one on a sunny day?	**4.** A black shirt will be hotter than a white one on a sunny day.

Did you notice that a hypothesis is always a statement, not a question? In fact, it is the answer to your experimental question.

The Null Hypothesis

Sometimes you want to say the opposite of what you think will happen. This is called a **null hypothesis.** For the sample projects, the null hypothesis would be:

- Battery A will not last longer than Batteries B, C, and D.
- Acid rain will not affect a plant's growth.
- Larger popcorn kernels will not produce larger popped popcorn.
- A gerbil cannot be taught to run a maze.
- A red feeder will not attract more hummingbirds than a white, blue, or green feeder.
- A black shirt will not be hotter than a white one on a sunny day.

Why do some scientists use a null hypothesis? Sometimes it is easier to disprove a statement than to prove it. You can choose to use either a hypothesis or a null hypothesis—it's up to you!

Prove It or Not

When you do the experiment, you will get an answer to your project question (the results), and you will also prove or disprove the hypothesis. Both steps are important parts of the scientific method. Proving the hypothesis or disproving the null hypothesis is the goal of the experiment.

Sometimes experiments do not turn out the way that researchers expect. In that case, they say they have *rejected the hypothesis*. It is okay to reject a hypothesis. It is also okay for an experiment to fail.

What is important is that you used the scientific method. Scientists understand that some of their experiments will not work as they expected them to, and that is part of the learning process. Did you know that penicillin was discovered through one such mistake?

5 Test Your Guess

Experimentation

Let's check your progress so far:

- You have selected a project.
- You have done some research into the background information for your topic.
- You have made a guess, a hypothesis.

Next, you need to plan how you are going to do the experiment.

A Recipe for Success: The Procedure

The plan for your experiment is called the **procedure.** It is a step-by-step guide to test your hypothesis. Think about the steps you'll need to take and the materials you'll need. Make your plan as detailed as possible. Imagine you are making a movie about your project and you are the director telling the actors what to do.

What is the "recipe" for your experiment? Write it down step by step in your logbook. Don't worry if you don't know exactly what you will need to do, or in what order. You can always fix it as you go. Use as many steps as you think you will need. How much time are you going to need to do your experiment? Can you do it in a few hours, or will it take days to see the results? Be sure you have enough time to do your experiment before the project is due!

Here are the procedures for our sample projects:

Sample #1

"Will Milk Spoil Faster If Left out of the Refrigerator?"

Step 1: Measure one cup of milk.

Step 2: Pour the milk into a jar. Cover with the lid.

Step 3: Place the jar in a box (to keep light out) and put it on a shelf in a cupboard.

Step 4: Put a thermometer next to the box.

Step 5: Measure another cup of milk.

Step 6: Pour the milk into another jar. Cover with the lid.

Step 7: Place the jar in a box and put it on a shelf in the refrigerator

Step 8: Put a thermometer next to the box.

Step 9: Check the jars every day at the same time of the day. Smell the milk. Look at its color and character. Check the temperature reading of each thermometer.

Step 10: In your logbook, write down each temperature and your observations each day.

Sample #2

"Which Battery Lasts Longer?"

Step 1: Place one Brand A battery into a flashlight and turn it on.

Step 2: With the stopwatch, time how long the battery lights the flashlight. Repeat this procedure for a second Brand A battery (with a second flashlight).

Step 3: Write down the times in the logbook.

Step 4: Repeat Steps 1 through 3 with each brand of battery.

"How Does Acid Rain Affect Plants?"

Step 1: Plant nine marigold seeds in nine pots of soil. Use the same bag of potting soil and make certain to plant the seeds at the same depth of soil. Mark today's date as Day 1 in your logbook.

Step 2: Give each potted plant one of the following labels: "Control 1," "Control 2," "Control 3," "Acidic 1," "Acidic 2," "Acidic 3," "Very Acidic 1," "Very Acidic 2," "Very Acidic 3."

Step 3: In a jar, mix vinegar with purified water. Use pH strips to test the acidity. Continue to add vinegar until the pH equals 4.5. Label this jar "Acidic."

Step 4: In another jar, mix more vinegar with purified water. Use pH strips to test the acidity. Continue to add vinegar until the pH equals 4.0. Label this jar "Very Acidic."

Step 5: Water the plants in each group by sprinkling the water over them as if it were rain. Use the amount of water recommended by a local nursery or plant guide. Be sure to give each plant the same amount of water. Water the plants in the control group with purified water (pH ~7.0) Water the plants in the acidic group with water from the "Acidic" jar (pH 4.5), and plants in the very acidic group with water from the "Very Acidic" jar (pH 4.0).

Step 6: Starting on the tenth day after planting, use a metric ruler to measure each plant's height from the soil to the top of the plant. Observe and record the color of the stem and leaves.

Step 7: Every five days after that, measure and record the height of each plant and your observations about the color and character of the stalk and leaves for each plant.

Controls and Variables

Every experiment needs a **control** subject or group and a **variable** subject or group (also known as the *test group*). The control is the subject or group of subjects against which the variable is compared. The variable subjects are the ones that are changed in the experiment. In

Sample #4

"Does the Largest Popcorn Kernel Produce the Largest Piece of Popped Popcorn?"

Step 1: Find the largest popcorn kernel in a bag or jar of unpopped popcorn. Using a metric ruler, measure the length of the kernel in millimeters.

Step 2: Pop this largest kernel in an air popper. Measure the popped popcorn and record the measurement.

Step 3: Pop 99 other kernels, one at a time. Measure their lengths before and after popping.

Step 4: Record all of your results in your logbook.

the plant experiment, for example, the control groups get pure water, while the variable groups get water with different levels of acidity.

The factors that you change on purpose in an experiment, to produce a certain result, are also known as variables. In the plant experiment, the variable is the level of the acidity of the water.

However, variables can also be other factors that are different between your control and experimental groups even though you didn't change them on purpose. These variables can not only affect your results but cause the experiment to fail.

For example, what other factors, or variables, might affect the plant project? What about light? What if you left one plant or group of plants in the shade and another in sunlight? Light is a variable that might affect the results of the experiment. You must make sure all of the plants get the same amount of light, at the same time of the day.

For this project, soil, temperature, air movement, the variety and age of the plant, and the amount of water can all affect a plant's growth. But you want to study only the effect of acid rain. To prevent the other variables from interfering with your project, be sure all of the plants are the same variety, and about the same size and age when you begin the experiment. Give them all the same amount of light, soil, temperature, and water. Keep them in a place where they will not be disturbed.

Sample variable

Project Question	Possible Variables
1. Which battery brand lasts longer?	• Age of batteries • Size of batteries (AA, AAA, etc.)
2. Does the largest popcorn kernel produce the largest piece of popped popcorn?	• Brand of popcorn used • Type of popcorn (blue corn, gourmet, etc.) • How the popcorn is stored
3. Which color attracts hummingbirds?	• Size of the feeding box • Type and amount of food
4. Is a black shirt hotter than a white one on a sunny day?	• Fabric of shirt • Size of shirt

These are just a few of the variables that might influence the outcome of these experiments. It is important to keep conditions for the control group and the test group as identical as possible, except for the factors you are changing for the experiment.

BRAINSTORM!

When you are working with two or more experimental subjects, it is important to keep the conditions that affect them as similar as possible. Try to identify the variables that might affect your experiment. What variables are you changing on purpose? What variables might ruin your experiment? How can you prevent variables from having an unwanted effect? What is your control? Write these down in your logbook.

Sometimes you have one control, as in the battery and popcorn projects. Other times you need to have several test subjects in the control group. For example, when you are working with plants, plan to have two or three in each group. Then you can average the growth or the change of all three plants so that individual sizes or rates of growth will not influence the results of the project. (For more on averaging, see Chapter 7.)

Safety

Another important aspect to consider as you design your procedure is safety. Will you be using chemicals? Electricity? Animals? Your project must not harm you, animals, or your little brother!

Consider where you'll do the experiment. Who can supervise you? Will you experiment at a science lab at school? At the hospital with a lab technician or a doctor who will be your mentor? At home in your kitchen?

You will need to think about any necessary safety precautions and include these in your procedure. For example, if you are collecting water from a river to test pollution, you may want to wear gloves. If you are popping popcorn in a hot-air popper, it's a good idea to wear goggles and oven mitts. Your teacher probably has a list of safety rules for the lab at school. He may also suggest safety guidelines for experimenting at home or another location.

Look at your procedure and think about any safety precautions you'll need to take. Write them down. Then ask your teacher or a parent to look at your procedure, paying special attention to safety.

Materials

After you've figured out what your procedure, control, and variables will be, you'll know what equipment and materials you need to do your project. You're now ready to compile a **materials list.**

BRAINSTORM!

In your logbook, write down the list of materials you will need for your experiment. Use your procedure as a guide. Don't worry if you forget something. You can add to this list as you work. Are any of the items going to be hard to find? Or too expensive? Be certain you know in advance where you're going to get the items and about how much they're going to cost.

Talk to your teacher or a parent if any materials are hard to find or too expensive. You may need to replace that item with something else. For example, in the plant experiment, perhaps 40 rose plants would cost too much, but 40 marigolds would be okay.

In addition to the obvious, such as popcorn for the popcorn project, don't forget things like:

- Electricity
- Water
- Sunlight
- Heat
- Cold
- Storage space
- Special equipment

Sample material lists

Sample #1

"Will Milk Spoil Faster If Left out of the Refrigerator?"

Materials:

1 carton of whole milk	2 glass jars with lids
refrigerator	2 Fahrenheit thermometers
1-cup measuring cup	2 cardboard boxes

Sample #2

"Which Battery Lasts Longest?"

Materials:

2 batteries each (same size) of 4 different brands of batteries

8 identical, brand-new flashlights that require only 1 battery each
stopwatch

Sample #3

"How Does Acid Rain Affect Plants?"

Materials:

9 pots	2 jars
marigold seeds	pH test strips
potting soil	measuring cup for watering
distilled white vinegar	marker for labeling pots
purified water	metric ruler

Sample #4

"Does the Largest Popcorn Kernel Produce the Largest Piece of Popped Popcorn?"

Materials:

bag or jar of unpopped popcorn (not microwave-type)	bowl
hot-air popcorn popper	metric ruler

Just Do It!

It is finally time to put your procedure into action! Remember to stick to your procedure, and try not to get distracted. (Experimenting can be so much fun that you may be tempted to keep on trying new experiments. You may want to know if Battery A will play a radio longer than lighting a bulb, or if different kinds of acid will affect plants differently. Go ahead and write these ideas down in your logbook, but for now just concentrate on finishing your current project.) If you find that you have time left before the science fair, you may want to repeat your experiment. This is known as another **trial.** Scientists often run multiple trials. That way they can see whether their results are reliable.

What If You Encounter Trouble?

What if something goes wrong with your experiment? What if your dog knocks over all of your plants? What if your results are completely different from what you expected?

Remember that it is okay to fail! (It is *not* okay to wait until the night before the fair to throw together an experiment.) Sometimes things happen that are beyond your control. If you have enough time, try again. If you are working at home, make certain to experiment in a location that will be undisturbed. Perhaps you can use a section of the garage or basement.

The important part of doing a project is learning about the scientific method. Scientists make mistakes too!

The completion of your experiment is not the end of the project! While you are experimenting, you also have to keep track of all of your results. Check the next chapter for tips on record-keeping.

If necessary, revise your procedure in your logbook until it's just the way you want it. Draw pictures or diagrams of steps if that makes them clearer.

Assisting in the Lab

Your child is ready to perform his science experiment. This will probably require some help from you in the form of supervision and financial resources. Older students may have a science laboratory available to them and even a small budget for their project. Most students, however, do their projects at home.

You can help by first reviewing your child's procedure and making certain that it is feasible and safe. You may need to suggest substitutes for expensive items. You might also be able to borrow equipment or lab space. The local high school or community college might be willing to let your budding Marie Curie use a Bunsen burner and microscope. A local nursery might donate plants or offer them at a reduced price. Be creative and don't be afraid to ask for help from your family doctor, that friend who is a vet, or your sister the engineer.

If your child is having problems getting his experiment to work, suggest that he check the variables. See whether you can help figure out if any variable is affecting the results. If he is experimenting at home, make sure he has a good place that is undisturbed by family traffic.

6 Write It Down

Recording Your Observations

As you experiment, you'll need to record what you observe and measure. These observations are known as your **data.** Some of this data will be descriptive. For example, in the acid rain experiment, you can observe and describe the color of the plants' leaves or stems. In the battery experiment, you might note how bright the light was or whether or not it flickered. These are called subjective, or **qualitative,** observations.

Other results will be measured and expressed in numbers rather than written down as descriptions. These are called objective, or **quantitative,** observations. For example, to study the effects of acid rain on plant growth, you would also measure the height of the plants to determine how much they grow over a certain period of time. If you were testing batteries, you would record the length of time each one keeps the lightbulb lit. To answer the question "Which popcorn will produce the largest popped popcorn?" you would measure each kernel before and after popping.

In all cases, it is helpful to create a place in your logbook to write down your results. As you record your observations, always remember to write down the type of measurements used. For example, temperature can be recorded in degrees Fahrenheit or Centigrade. Which type of thermometer are you using? Length can be measured in millimeters, centimeters, or inches. Which type of ruler are you using?

It is best to use metric measurements because these are used by all scientists. The ruler you have at home or in school may not include metric measurements. Your teacher should be able to help you get a metric ruler. Be sure you always use the same ruler or scale or thermometer to measure the results of your experiment. It is also important to measure at the same time of day each time. The time of day could be a variable in your experiment.

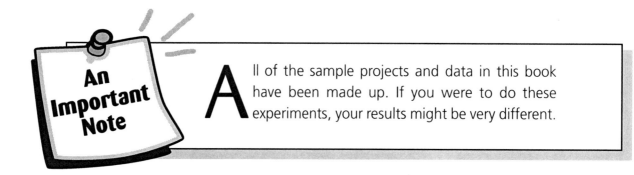

An Important Note

All of the sample projects and data in this book have been made up. If you were to do these experiments, your results might be very different.

Tables

Whether the results that you've recorded are qualitative or quantitative, you need an organized system for recording them. You don't want your results to get lost among other entries in your logbook. The best way to record your observations is to construct a table. You can tell at a glance what happened in a project by reading the table.

Begin with the control subject or group. Then compare the variable subject or group to it.

"Which Battery Lasts Longer?"				
	Battery A	Battery B	Battery C	Battery D
Length of time	2 hr., 13 min.	2 hr., 4 min.	1 hr.	2 hr., 9 min.

The time has been recorded in hours and minutes (using a stopwatch or clock). To make working with the results easier, you might want to convert all of the time into minutes. Then the table would look like this:

"Which Battery Lasts Longer?"				
	Battery A	Battery B	Battery C	Battery D
Length of time	133 min.	124 min.	60 min.	129 min.

Setting up a Table

A table always needs a title. You can use your experimental question as the title. What you are observing is listed on the left side, and the test subjects are listed across the top of the table.

In the sample project on the growth of plants affected by acid rain, the table would look like this:

"How Does Acid Rain Affect the Growth of Plants?"				
Solutions	Growth Day 1	Growth Day 10	Growth Day 15	Growth Day 20
Purified water (control— pH ~7.0)				
Plant 1	0 cm	1 cm	6 cm	14 cm
Plant 2	0 cm	1.5 cm	7 cm	14.5 cm
Plant 3	0 cm	1.3 cm	6.4 cm	14.2 cm
Acidic water (pH 4.5)				
Plant 1	0 cm	0 cm	3 cm	8 cm
Plant 2	0 cm	.8 cm	2.7 cm	7.8 cm
Plant 3	0 cm	1.0 cm	3 cm	7.5 cm
Very acidic water (pH 4.0)				
Plant 1	0 cm	0 cm	1 cm	0 cm
Plant 2	0 cm	0.2 cm	0.8 cm	0 cm
Plant 3	0 cm	0.5 cm	0.4 cm	0 cm

The plants took ten days to germinate, so they were measured on Day 10. After that, they were measured again every five days. (Plants grow too slowly to measure them every day.) If you were doing this experiment, it would be important to use the same brand throughout the experiment, because the pH of purified water ranges from 7.0 to 7.8, depending on the brand. You would also want to remember to measure the pH of the purified water for the control group.

For this project, you could also make qualitative observations in your logbook, such as noting that the third test group had died by Day

20, or that the leaves on the plants in the second group became much yellower and browner than the control's leaves. A table for these observations might look like this:

"How Does Acid Rain Affect the Growth of Plants?"				
Solutions	Day 1	Day 10	Day 15	Day 20
Purified water (control—pH ~7.0)				
Plant 1		Leaves starting to grow, very green	Leaves full and green, stem very straight	Leaves even bigger, still dark green
Plant 2		Same as 1	Same as 1	Same as 1
Plant 3		Same as 1	Same as 1	Same as 1
Acidic water (pH 4.5)				
Plant 1		No growth yet	Leaves showing brown spots	Some leaves withered and brown
Plant 2		Some small leaves, more yellowish in color	Same as 1	Same as 1
Plant 3		Same as 2	Same as 1	Same as 1
Very acidic water (pH 4.0)				
Plant 1		No growth	Stem withered	Dead
Plant 2		No leaves	Same as 1	Same as 1
Plant 3		No leaves	Same as 1	Same as 1

You might want to continue growing and observing the control group and plants given acidic water for several weeks.

For the popcorn project, your table would have 100 columns (one for each kernel studied). You may not think that is practical, but that is the way a scientist would record the data!

Remember that the results here are just examples. If you do these projects, your results will be different.

Will your observations be qualitative or quantitative, or both? Make a table in your logbook to record your results. Be certain to include the types of measurement you are using (degrees Fahrenheit, centimeters, etc.).

Tips on Recording Your Observations

1. Record your observations in some form of a table, but keep qualitative and quantitative observations separate. Writing your observations in different places or on different pages of your logbook makes it hard to use the information later. Create tables before you even begin writing down the results of your experiment.

2. Write your observations down as soon as you have made them. You won't remember them otherwise. Scraps of paper will be lost. Write them in pen, not in pencil. If you make a mistake, simply cross it out instead of erasing it. Then write the correct information.

3. Be as consistent as possible. If you are measuring every day, don't skip a day. Measure at the same time each day. Decide ahead of time when this will be to make sure you'll always be available at that time of day to make a measurement. Always use the exact same measurement tool, not just the same type of tool. Scales and thermometers can differ from one to the next.

A Picture Is Worth a Thousand Words

Here's a great idea: Take a picture or video of your results! You can use the photos or a video later in your display. Photos are often the best way to show qualitative results to others.

Be creative in making your observations. You may want to draw a picture or even tape-record your results. For example, if you are testing which brand of soda your classmates prefer, you might record their responses on video- or audiotape.

However, remember that in addition to these methods of recording results, you'll still need to write your qualitative and quantitative observations down in tables in your logbook.

Even though you've done your experiment and recorded the results, you're not finished yet. (But you are getting really close!) Next, you will need to take a closer look at the results. What do they really mean? How can you show your teacher and the judges at the science fair what your results mean? In the next chapter, we'll discuss ways you can display your results by using graphs.

Stay Supportive

Be sure your child knows how to use the appropriate measurement device for her project. She may need your help the first couple of times to use the measuring tool accurately and record the correct results.

If the results of her experiment show early on that her hypothesis is not going to be supported, help her to not become discouraged. Remind her that not all experiments turn out the way scientists think they will. Failing to support the hypothesis does not mean that she has failed in the project.

7 Get It All Together

Organizing Your Data

So far you have taken the quantitative or qualitative observations (data) from your experiment and created tables. Now you're going to use those tables to create meaningful pictures, or **graphs,** to display your data.

Graphs help you see patterns in your data so that you can form conclusions about the results of your experiment. Graphs also allow your teacher and the judges at the science fair to understand your results quickly and easily.

You don't want to use a graph just for the sake of having one in your display. There are lots of different kinds of graphs, and you should choose the one that will best show your results. The kind of graph you use may depend on your data. Let's consider the data from the sample projects.

Showing Qualitative Results

Believe it or not, some results just can't be graphed. For example, the qualitative results observed in the plant project can't be plotted on a graph. Instead, you might type the table from your logbook or print it neatly and display it on your backboard. Make it large enough to be read easily. If you took photographs of the plants, you might also want to display them to show your qualitative observations.

If you have chosen an experiment that involves making qualitative observations, don't worry that you're the only student at the fair without a graph on your backboard! Understanding the difference between quantitative and qualitative data may actually impress a judge! And remember, you never want to make a graph for the sake of making a graph. It needs to make sense.

So when should you graph your data? What kind of graph should you use?

Showing Quantitative Results

In the battery experiment, two batteries of each brand were loaded into individual flashlights so that two tests (also called **runs,** or **trials**) of the experiment could be done. Then two sets of data tables were created.

For a more complex project, you could use four or six batteries of each brand for several runs. Scientists sometimes perform the same experiment hundreds of times. That way they know that one test subject won't affect their results.

The only problem with using multiple test groups is that you get a lot of data. You don't want to have to display all of the tables, so a graph is helpful in this situation because it allows you to show how all of the batteries you tested compare to the control (Brand A).

What Is an Average?

First, you need to find **averages.** The best way to treat data when you have multiple test groups, whether two or two hundred, is to *use the average.*

You've heard of averages before. Maybe when your teacher passes back tests she announces the average grade of the class. Or perhaps you play baseball and have a good batting average.

Suppose you tested two of each brand of battery. You would make a table for each battery, like this:

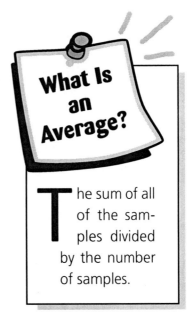

What Is an Average?

The sum of all of the samples divided by the number of samples.

"Which Battery Lasts Longer?"				
	Battery A1	Battery B1	Battery C1	Battery D1
Length of time	133 min.	124 min.	60 min.	129 min.

	Battery A2	Battery B2	Battery C2	Battery D2
Length of time	140 min.	122 min.	76 min.	120 min.

If you used more batteries than this, you would call the next set Battery A3, B3, C3, and D3, etc.

Next, add the number of minutes of Batteries A1 and A2 and, since you used two batteries, divide by 2 to obtain the average length of time the batteries of that brand lasted. The average length, then, of Battery A would be:

$$\frac{133 + 140}{2}$$

or 136.5 minutes. Let's average the rest of the battery brands:

"Which Battery Lasts Longest?": Averages

	Battery A	Battery B	Battery C	Battery D
Average length of time	136.5 min.	123 min.	68 min.	124.5 min.

f you used multiple test groups or did the project several times (multiple runs), average your data for each group and record the averages in a table in your logbook. Be sure to mark the table "Averages" to keep it from being confused with the experimental data tables.

Bar Graphs

Bar graphs are the best choice when you want to show differences between similar experimental subjects. A bar graph shows data with side-by-side columns. To make a bar graph for the battery project, you would record intervals of time along the left side of the graph. Along the bottom of the graph you would list the subjects, Battery A, Battery B, Battery C, and Battery D.

Tips for Making a Bar Graph

1. Title your graph. You may use the title of the project or a title that explains what the graph is all about. What does the graph show?

2. Label the two axes clearly. The line going up and down is the *vertical axis*. The line across is the *horizontal axis.*

3. Make sure the scale for the numbers you use along one axis is reasonable. The interval between the numbers should be consistent, and the scale should include the smallest and largest data. For example, you have recorded the time in minutes, so start with 0 and increase by 20-minute intervals. You don't want to start with 0 and go up by 5 minutes, then skip to 20, then go to 15; keep each interval equal. Go beyond the longest time you recorded. If you are using a computer graphing program, the program should automatically do this for you.

4. If you are not using a computer program, make your graph by using different colors of construction paper or marking pens. If each column is a different color, it's easy to see the differences between them.

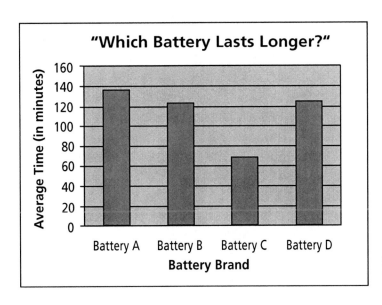

Sample bar graph.

Line Graphs

What if in your comparison of the differences between several things you need to show *change* in each subject over time? In that case, you would use a *line graph*. Line graphs are used to demonstrate trends over a period of time. The student studying acid rain and plants, for example, might choose to make a line graph from that kind of data. First average the results for the three test groups of plants used:

"How Does Acid Rain Affect Plants?": Average Growth

Acidity	Height of Plants Day 1	Height of Plants Day 10	Height of Plants Day 15	Height of Plants Day 20
pH 6.0 (purified water)	0 cm	1.27 cm	6.47 cm	14.23 cm
pH 4.0 (acidic)	0 cm	0.9 cm	2.9 cm	7.8 cm
pH 3.0 (very acidic)	0 cm	0.23 cm	0.73 cm	0 cm

Follow the same steps outlined earlier—title your graph and draw the scale to include the highest and lowest values. Then make each measurement a point on the graph and play connect-the-dots!

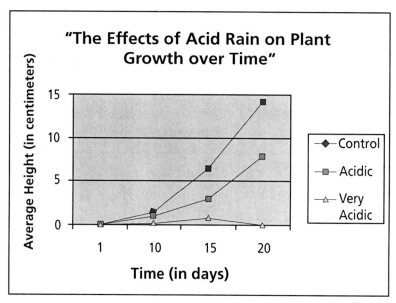

Sample line graph.

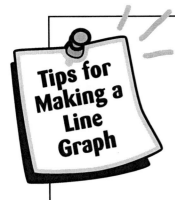

Tips for Making a Line Graph

1. Title your graph. What are you showing?

2. Label the two axes (the horizontal and vertical sides of the graph) clearly.

3. Make sure the scale or measurements are reasonable and consistent.

4. If you are graphing by hand, draw dots at the appropriate points for each observation.

5. Using a ruler, connect the points with straight lines. Use different colors of marking pens (one color for each group) to show the differences clearly.

Pie Charts

What if you studied which color attracts hummingbirds? Perhaps you set up several feeders of different colors and counted how many hummingbirds visited each one. Then you made a table for each color and listed the number of birds that visited that feeder. Perhaps you did this for several days and then averaged those numbers to come up with one number for each color of feeder.

For your graph you want to show how many birds out of the total number you saw visited each feeder. A *pie chart* is just what you need. Pie charts are used to demonstrate how the total amount of something is divided.

For the hummingbird experiment, your data table might look like this:

"Which Color Attracts the Most Hummingbirds?"				
	Green	Blue	White	Red
Number of hummingbird visits	5 birds	4 birds	3 birds	8 birds

You saw a total of 20 hummingbirds (5 + 4 + 3 + 8 = 20). Of the 20 observations, 5 were made at the blue feeder. So $\frac{5}{20}$ (¼ when reduced) of the total observations were made at the blue feeder. In percentages, this is expressed as 25 percent. So the slice of the pie that represents the blue feeder would be 25 percent of the whole pie. You would do the same with all of the other colors, and your pie chart would look like this:

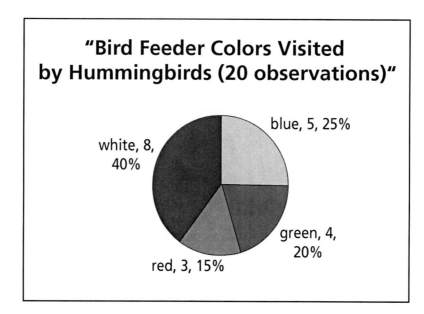

"Bird Feeder Colors Visited by Hummingbirds (20 observations)"

blue, 5, 25%

white, 8, 40%

green, 4, 20%

red, 3, 15%

Sample pie chart.

Tips for Making a Pie Chart

1. Title your pie chart. Remember, you can use the title of your project or something else. What are you showing?

2. Determine the total number that the complete pie chart represents (in this case, the total number of observations of hummingbird visits).

3. If you are drawing by hand, you'll need a *circular protractor* to draw a perfect circle. Ask your teacher or a parent for this tool. Divide the circle into equal parts, according to the number of observations. For 20, for example, you would divide the circle into 20 equal sections. Again, you might need some help with this step.

4. Determine the proportion. What part of the pie does each subject get? If 5 birds out of 20 visited the blue feeder, you would fill in 5 of the equal 20 segments of the pie chart with one color. Do this for all of the data, making the section for each subject a different color.

5. Be sure to also label each of the different sections with the numeric proportion, or percentage.

Now that you understand the different kinds of graphs, choose the best one for your project. You can transform your tables of data into pictures. Remember to make them neat and colorful, and choose wisely when deciding what type of graph you will use!

Graphing is usually not easy, but it is important because graphs are a visual picture of your data. The visual piece, however, is only a part of the whole report you're going to do on the project. The next step is to write a description of everything you've learned and done.

Look at your data. What kind of graph should you use? Remember that for some qualitative results graphs are not practical.

Avoid Taking Over

Your child may need your help with the graphing process, but be sure to avoid taking over the task for him. Making graphs is hard work, especially if your child is doing one by hand. But even when using a computer program, he needs to do most of the work himself in order to understand how to put the information into the program correctly and what he hopes to show.

You may need to sit down with your child and go through the steps of making a graph or using the software to make graphs. You can also take the time to demonstrate to your child how to find the average of his data, or the ratio of a part to the whole if he is making a pie chart. However, when it comes to setting up actual spreadsheets or putting marker to poster board, you need to fade into the background again.

8 Pick up the Pieces

The Research Paper

Do it. Show it. Tell it. Those are the basics of a science fair project.

Now it's time for the "show it" phase. You're going to write a paper about your project. You've actually been working on your paper all along. Since you've been keeping careful notes on index cards and in your logbook, you'll find that writing the research paper is easy! All you have to do is put together all of the work you've done.

As with the organization of a science fair project, there's a basic format you can follow for organizing your written report. Start with the title of your project and what you expected to learn from your experiment. That's right, the **hypothesis** and the **purpose.** Then add a section summarizing the background information you discovered from your research. List your experimental procedure, step by step, and describe your results, including your tables and graphs. Finally, write your conclusions. Did your experiment prove (support) your hypothesis?

Basic Research Paper Outline

Title

Hypothesis

Purpose

Background

Materials list

Procedure

Results

Conclusions

Bibliography

Sounds easy, right? Well, just to be sure, we'll go through each section of the paper and describe the kind of information that should go in each one.

Plagiarism

Plagiarism is a serious offense. Explain to your child that if she did something for which she could be rewarded, she would be very upset if someone else took credit for her work. Plagiarism is the same thing. An idea cannot be owned, but the words that express that idea belong to the person who said or wrote them. An occasional short direct quote is okay, so long as the child learns how to properly cite the quotation.

For the older child, a teacher may provide specific guidelines for **citations.** There are three widely accepted methods of citation:

● Parenthetical citation

● Footnotes

● Endnotes

Most important, however, remind your child that her paper should not be a series of quotations from the sources but a summary of what she has learned, in her own words. You can help by discussing her project with her, what she has learned from her research, and how she plans to use the information she has found.

Pen or Keyboard?

Should you hand-write your paper or use a computer? That question is up to your teacher, but it also depends on whether you have access to and know how to use a word-processing program.

If you use a computer, there are some general formatting guidelines. First, no cutting and pasting from other sources. Whether you are using a computer or copying by hand, this is known as **plagiarism.** It also doesn't matter whether the information came from Internet resources or from books or magazine articles from the library. Although it is tempting to copy, plagiarism is wrong. You must write the paper in your own words.

For the **format** (the way the paper is set up), use a standard font type and size, such as Times New Roman, size 12. Research papers are usually double-spaced with margins of one inch.

If you hand-write your paper, write with a pen unless the teacher instructs you otherwise, use school loose-leaf paper, and write on every other line. This makes it neater and easier for the teacher to read. For both computer and handwritten papers, use only the front of each sheet and put the whole paper into a plastic report cover. You may need to write a rough draft of the paper and then recopy it to make sure it's neat and has no erasures.

Title, Hypothesis, and Purpose

The first sentence after the title and hypothesis should describe why you wanted to do this project or how you chose it.

"How Does Acid Rain Affect Plants?"

Hypothesis
Plants exposed to acid rain will take longer to grow.

Purpose
I've read that acid rain is bad for plants. I like to garden. I wanted to find out how acid rain affects the way plants grow.

Background

Next, write a summary of the background information you found in your research. Remember to write it in your own words. This is where those index cards come in handy. You can spread them out on the table or floor in front of you according to their key words. Then, after you use the information on each one, put it aside. At the end, you can copy the information about the sources from the backs of the cards. This will be your bibliography.

The background information for the sample project might look like this:

"How Does Acid Rain Affect Plants?"

Background

When fossil fuels such as coal, oil, and natural gas are burned, pollution is released into the atmosphere. Common kinds of pollution include sulfur dioxide and nitrogen oxides. When these mix with water vapor and sunlight, sulfuric and nitric acid are created. These become part of water vapor in clouds and eventually precipitate. This is known as acid rain. It may also fall as snow, sleet, fog, mist, or hail.

These acids can harm plants when they get into the leaves through pores (small holes). In fact, according to atmospheric scientist Jonathan Kahl, "In the United States, this pollution destroys $2-5 billion in crops each year and reduces food production by 5-10 percent."

You probably won't use all of the information from your background research in your paper. You'll need to determine what information is necessary and what you can leave out.

Materials List and Procedure

Next, write down the materials list and the procedure, step by step.

Notice that the materials list and the procedure differ slightly from those written down before the actual experiment. Sometimes as you are working on an experiment you realize that you missed a step or that other materials are needed. You can add those to your procedure now.

"How Does Acid Rain Affect Plants?"

Materials

9 pots	2 jars
tomato seeds	pH test strips
potting soil	measuring cup for watering
distilled white vinegar	marker for labeling pots
purified water	metric ruler

"How Does Acid Rain Affect Plants?"

Procedure

Step 1: Plant nine tomato seeds in nine pots of soil.

Step 2: Give each potted plant one of the following labels: "Control 1," "Control 2," "Control 3," "Acidic 1," "Acidic 2," "Acidic 3," "Very Acidic 1," "Very Acidic 2," "Very Acidic 3."

Step 3: In a jar, mix some vinegar with purified water. Use pH strips to test the acidity. Continue to add vinegar until the pH equals 4.5. Label this jar "Acidic."

Step 4: In another jar, mix more vinegar with purified water. Use pH strips to test the acidity. Continue to add vinegar until the pH equals 4.0. Label this jar "Very Acidic."

Step 5: Water plants in each group using the frequency and amount recommended by a local nursery or plant guide. Be sure to give each plant the same amount of water. Water plants in the control group with purified water (pH ~7.0). Water plants in the acidic group with water from the "Acidic" jar (pH 4.5), and plants in the very acidic group with water from the "Very Acidic" jar (pH 4.0).

Step 6: Using a metric ruler, measure each plant's height from the soil to the top of the plant on Day 10, and then every five days after that.

Step 7: Also record observations of the color and character of the stalk and leaves for each plant.

Results

After the procedure, you can write the **results.** First, describe your observations, then state the measurements you used to determine your results.

You can copy the tables from your logbook and put them in this section of the paper. Add a copy of the graphs you made, and the paper is almost finished! These last two items will also appear on your backboard or display, but it's still a good idea to include them in your paper. This makes a complete record of all you have done from start to finish.

Remember, it is okay when a project does not support or prove the hypothesis. Some experiments do not turn out the way you expect them to. The most important part is that you followed the scientific method, and you are following it again now in your paper.

Conclusions

In the last part of your paper, state the **conclusions** you formed because of your experiment. Explain why you think the results of your experiment proved (supported) your hypothesis or rejected it.

Be sure to restate your hypothesis in the conclusion. And remember that it's okay when a project does not prove or support the hypothesis. Some experiments do not turn out the way you expect them to. The most important part is that you followed the scientific method.

The Bibliography

Next, you need to include your sources of background information. Remember that, on the backs of the index cards, you wrote down the name of every author and book or magazine article that you consulted. Now you need to do something with that information. You're going to write a bibliography for your paper.

The items in a bibliography are always in alphabetical order according to the author's last name. Go back to your index cards, sort through them, and put them in that order. (See Chapter 3 for samples of how to write the information for the bibliography.)

When you have written the bibliography, you are done with the paper. Give yourself a pat on the back.

Finishing Touches

Writing the paper is often the hardest part of the project, and you're done with that. Congratulations! You've finished the basics of your paper. But there's still a little more to do.

"How Does Acid Rain Affect Plants?"

Conclusions

The plants that were given acidic water (pH 4.5) grew more slowly than the control. The plants that were given very acidic water (pH 4.0) grew most slowly and died by Day 15. Therefore, the hypothesis that acid rain will cause plants to grow more slowly was accepted.

Checking your work

Your job now is to be a detective. Search for spelling mistakes, missing words, and lost credits for sources. What are the easiest mistakes to make? How can you catch them? Here are a few common errors to look for when you read through your paper.

"Affect"/"effect." These two words cause science fair students no end of trouble. Remember that "affect" is a verb that states that a change is occurring. For example, "How Weather Affects Plants" is correct.

"Effect," on the other hand, is a noun that describes the result of that change. For example, "The Effect of Rain on Plants" uses "effect" correctly.

Spelling. If you are using a computer, catching spelling errors should be easy, right? Not always. The computer spell-checker function can catch many spelling errors, but not all. For example, there are three correct ways to spell the word "to": "to," "two," and "too." The computer can recognize a misspelled word but doesn't know which word you intended to use. You must read what you have written to catch errors. Even then, you may miss mistakes because you know what you intended to write and your brain may skip right over a mistake. Have someone else read your paper. Hint: Be sure that person is a good speller!

It is also helpful to read your paper aloud. Sometimes you will hear a mistake that you didn't see. Since the paper is your teacher's main way (or maybe only way) of knowing what you did and whether you followed the scientific method, it will probably be what she uses to give you a grade for the project. Make your paper as perfect as possible.

PARENTS

Is It Time Yet?

Ah, the temptation to step in and help may be greatest now, when your child has to write a paper. You could do it so much faster and easier. You won't make spelling mistakes. You know to include a verb in every sentence. Everyone can read your handwriting.

Don't do it.

Experimentation is fun. Designing the display is creative. Writing the paper is hard. Making tables is even more difficult. But they're all critical steps in the lesson of following through with a project.

You can still help your child, though. You can suggest ways to organize the material so that the paper makes sense. And you can read through the paper when it's finished and correct spelling and grammatical errors. That's about it.

When you read the paper, use the sandwich method of criticism: Slide a slice of criticism between two pieces of praise. And be sure to use the completion of the paper as an opportunity for a celebration. The project is almost done. Your kitchen is no longer a science lab. The science fair is a couple of days away, and your child is going for the gold!

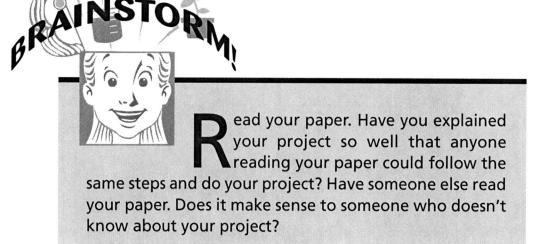

How Long Should the Paper Be?

Here's a good rule: Your paper should be as long as it needs to be. You want your teacher and the science fair judge to see what you did, why you did it, and the results you got. You need to include some background information, but not everything you have learned on the subject. You should include the materials list, the procedure, and the results, in the form of both subjective (if any) and objective observations, and the tables you have made to illustrate your results. If you have gone a step further and made graphs, put them in the paper also.

You can accomplish all of this in three pages, or you may need thirty or more pages. Be as thorough and neat as you can.

The Abstract

Some teachers will want you to write what is called an **abstract.** (If you go on with science fair projects in junior or senior high, this will be a requirement.) An abstract is a very short explanation of your entire project, usually in one or two paragraphs and fewer than 250 words. It gives anyone looking at your project a quick explanation of it. You may wonder how you will rewrite a twenty-page paper in a couple of paragraphs, but it isn't really all that hard.

Begin with the hypothesis again. Summarize the background information in one or two sentences. Instead of including the complete

Sample Abstract

"How Does Acid Rain Affect Plants?"

Abstract

Acid rain is a serious problem in the United States. It is caused by the burning of fossil fuels, which creates air pollution. This pollution mixes with water vapor and sunlight in the earth's atmosphere and falls to the ground in the form of rain or other precipitation.

The purpose of this project was to determine the effects of acid rain on tomato plants. It was hypothesized that plants exposed to acidic water would grow more slowly. Nine tomato plants were grown from seed. Three were given purified water as a control. Three were given acidic water (pH 4.5). Three were given very acidic water (pH 4.0). The plants' growth was observed every fifth day for twenty days.

The plants that were given acidic water grew more slowly than the control. The plants that were given very acidic water grew most slowly and actually died by Day 15. Therefore, the hypothesis was accepted.

Miller, Christina. *Acid Rain: A Sourcebook for Young People*. Simon & Schuster: NY, 1986.

Baines, John. *Acid Rain*. Steck-Vaughn Library: TX, 1990.

procedure for the project, explain how you did the project and what the results were in a sentence or two, and add the conclusion at the end. You will also want to list the two most important resources from the bibliography.

Put your research paper in a three-ring binder or a plastic cover, according to your teacher's instructions. Now let's head for the next destination on our science fair trip: the display.

Helpful Reference Books

So what do you do if your own paper-writing skills are rusty? There are several excellent books you might consider adding to your home library because they will serve your student well throughout his high school and college careers. *The Chicago Manual of Style* (University of Chicago Press, 14th ed., 1993) is a complete reference for grammar, spelling, source citation, and editing. *The Modern Language Association Handbook for Writers of Research Papers* (Modern Language Association of America, 1995) is another reference used more often in science writing. *Woe Is I* by Patricia T. O'Connor (Gossett-Putnam Publishers, 1996) makes grammar so much fun that you can enjoy simply reading it.

9 Show It Off

The Backboard

As you've been learning, doing a science fair project requires that you follow certain steps, in their proper order. So far you have been concentrating on using the scientific method to research an idea and perform an experiment. Now it's time to switch gears and use your creativity and artistic skills to plan a display for the science fair. You may think this is the easiest part of the project. All you have to do is buy the poster board and write on it with a marking pen, right?

Actually, there's a lot more that goes into making a great display for your project.

Planning is the first step.

What does a grocery store display have to do with your science fair project? Many of the qualities of any great display can help you show off your project. Remember, you want to attract the judges just like a store wants to attract customers.

What makes a good display? Think about what attracts your attention to a billboard, a magazine ad, a television commercial, or a store display. What makes a display less effective? Write in your logbook what you think works and what doesn't.

An effective display is	An ineffective display is
• well organized	• disorganized
• colorful and attractive	• too bright or too light
• easy to read from a distance	• hard to read
• well planned, with space for the words or pictures	• crowded with too little space between words or pictures
• free of spelling and grammatical errors	• full of misspelled words or other mistakes

As you plan your display, keep these qualities in mind. You've done a lot of hard work to this point. Your display is your way of showing all that work to your classmates, your teacher, and the science fair judges. You want to create a display that is organized, complete, and attractive. This sounds challenging, but it's easy when you break it down into steps.

The Display

When you plan your display, the first thing that comes to your mind is the **backboard.** That is a very important part of the display, but you can also include many other things, such as drawings, models, or photographs.

Don't worry, however, if all you have is a backboard. You can make a very effective display with that alone. You never want to add other things just for the sake of having a lot to display.

This chapter focuses on making a backboard. The other elements of the display will be covered in Chapter 10.

What Is a Backboard?

A backboard is simply a board used to show your work. It is usually made of cardboard, wood, or some other material, and it has three panels. Your teacher will probably give you size guidelines. Pay special attention to the size of your backboard. If yours is even a half-inch too wide, you could be disqualified.

Why do you want a three-paneled board? First, the panels can be adjusted to allow the backboard to stand independently. A single piece of cardboard or poster board needs to be hung or set against an easel. Second, the panels provide a lot of space and make it easy to organize the information you want to share about your project.

Cardboard Backboards

Most students use a three-paneled piece of cardboard that can be purchased at office supply stores, or sometimes through the school. The benefit of this type of backboard is that it is inexpensive, easy to use, and easy to transport. However, cardboard backboards are not durable, and often they are smaller than the maximum size allowed for a backboard. The cardboard or foam-core display board available in

Tips for Working with a Cardboard or Foam-core Backboard

- Buy two or three so that you have extras in case you make a mistake.

- Lay everything out first before you start writing anything on the board or stick letters to it.

- Always work in pencil, and have a good eraser handy.

most office supply stores is 36 inches by 48 inches. If you have a lot of data, graphs, or photographs, you may not have enough room on a cardboard backboard.

Do not write directly on the board, whether it is cardboard, wood, or foam-core. If you make a mistake, it can be very hard to fix. Instead, consider these options:

- Write on a piece of poster board, cut it to the correct size, then glue it to the backboard.

- If you must write on the board itself, draw lines and do everything in pencil first, then go over the writing with a marker. The goal is to have a perfect backboard with no spelling errors, blotches, or erasures.

Building Your Own Backboard

If you plan to continue to compete in science fairs in the future, or if you have younger brothers and sisters who could also use your backboard, you may want to consider building one that will last for several years. It is actually easier than it sounds to build a backboard of plywood, particle wood, or pegboard, and these are far more durable than cardboard or foam-core.

If you build your own backboard, the material should be durable, lightweight, and strong enough to stand independently. Again, be sure to observe carefully the dimensions allowed for the backboard to keep from being disqualified.

When working with corkboard, pegboard, or plywood, you will need some sort of hardware to attach the panels. Each of the side panels should be a little less than one-half the width of the back panel so that when attached with hinges, they fold flat against the back for easy carrying and storing.

Backboard Building for Beginners

Now you can definitely help, even if you aren't an expert in carpentry! You don't need to have a full workshop in your garage to build a plywood backboard. Most lumberyards will cut the wood to your dimensions, for free or for a small fee. Ask someone there for advice on what kind of hinges and screws you'll need to put the panels together. When you assemble the pieces, be sure to put the hinges on the front side of the panels so that the sides fold in toward the center.

You may also need to help your child cover the backboard with felt. Fabric stores carry felt that is sixty inches wide and comes in attractive colors. Stick with a dark one that doesn't show dirt. A lint brush works well if it does get dirty. Cut the felt a couple of inches larger than the panels, and *after* the board is assembled, stretch the felt across each panel and around the corners. Staple in place. You can cut around the hinges.

Decorating the wood is simple. It can be painted or covered with felt. Felt stapled to the board makes an excellent surface for a display. Use heavy stock or cardboard and double-faced tape to mount all of the information to the fabric-covered board. When the fair is over, you can carefully pull everything off and reuse the board next year.

Backboard Blues

No matter what type of material you use to build your backboard, be prepared by asking yourself questions about some of the common problems that can happen to any backboard. Think about your answers and how you can make sure that the worst doesn't happen to your backboard.

- How will I get the backboard to the science fair? Could it be damaged when I move it?
- How will the backboard hold up if I have to load and unload it in rain, wind, or snow?
- Can attachments such as graphs, drawings, or photographs come unglued?
- Can the backboard stand upright independently for many hours?

All That Space

Don't panic! You're going to fill all that space and probably wish you had more! Some extra space between elements makes the backboard easier to read. Remember the characteristics of an effective display? Be sure you have a good balance between the items on the backboard and the space between them.

There's a method to putting together the backboard, and it follows the scientific method that you have been using all along.

First, what do you need to have on the backboard?

Your teacher may have guidelines for what goes where, but if you didn't receive any instructions, you can use this approach. On the left-hand panel, at the top, state the purpose of the project. In the middle of the left-hand panel, show the hypothesis, and at the bottom your abstract (if you have one).

On the center panel, at the top, put your title. Beneath that go the tables of data from the experimentation, plus any graphs you made or photos of the project. At the bottom of that section, put the list of

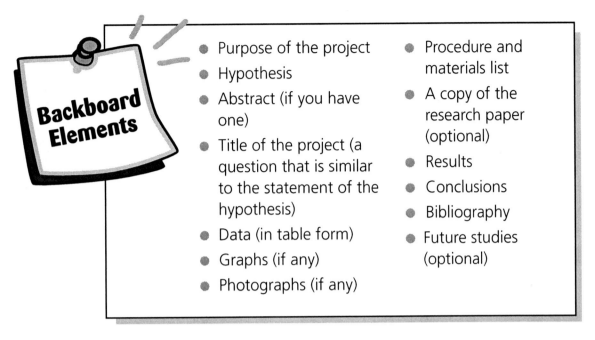

Backboard Elements

- Purpose of the project
- Hypothesis
- Abstract (if you have one)
- Title of the project (a question that is similar to the statement of the hypothesis)
- Data (in table form)
- Graphs (if any)
- Photographs (if any)
- Procedure and materials list
- A copy of the research paper (optional)
- Results
- Conclusions
- Bibliography
- Future studies (optional)

materials and the procedure. Some students add a copy of their research paper here.

To attach multiple pages, simply stack the pages of the paper as you would if you were handing it to someone. Attach the back of the last page to a mat. A glue stick is the easiest adhesive to use. Put a half-inch-wide line of glue along the top edge of the back of each page of the paper, then position each page in a stack on top of the last page. The top edges of the pages are all glued to each other and you can lift the pages to read the paper.

On the right-hand panel, at the top, add the results of the experiment. In the center, place your conclusions (whether or not the hypothesis was supported), and at the bottom of the panel your bibliography of the sources you used. Some students also like to add a statement of future plans to continue studying or experimenting.

Putting It All Together

Creating mats is a technique that works well no matter what type of backboard you have. Made from poster board of any color other than white, mats create an attractive background for your work. Any color is fine, and you can even use a different color for each section of the board as long as the colors are complementary. Just be careful about using neon colors. They can be hard on the eyes and might bother the judges.

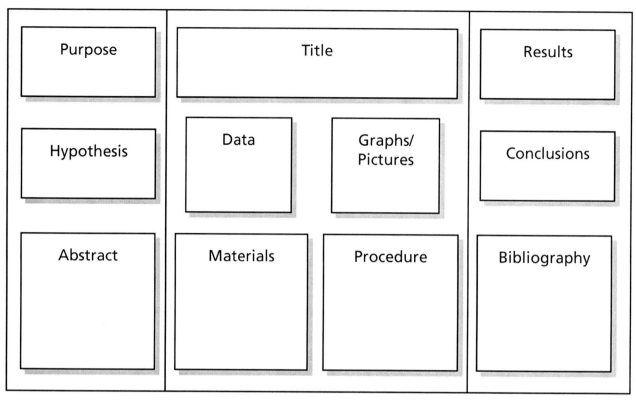

Purpose	Title	Results
Hypothesis	Data / Graphs/Pictures	Conclusions
Abstract	Materials / Procedure	Bibliography

Sample layout for a backboard.

When you use a mat, you don't have to hand-write anything. You can print all of your information using a computer or typewriter, trim the paper with a paper cutter, and then glue the pages to a mat. Using a mat gives you some color so that you don't have white paper on a white background.

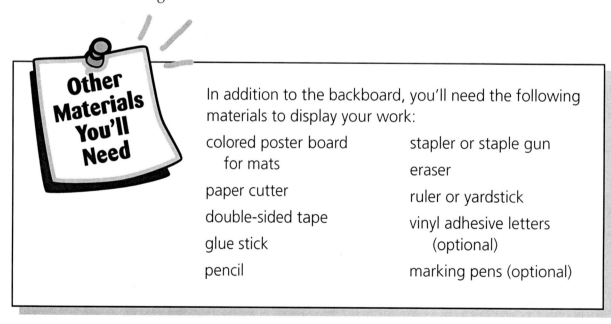

Other Materials You'll Need

In addition to the backboard, you'll need the following materials to display your work:

colored poster board for mats

paper cutter

double-sided tape

glue stick

pencil

stapler or staple gun

eraser

ruler or yardstick

vinyl adhesive letters (optional)

marking pens (optional)

Using mats is easy when you think about the elements of your backboard as either whole sheets or half-sheets. For example, your purpose and hypothesis are brief statements. They will need only a half-page. Your abstract and procedure are longer, taking up a full page. Other elements of the display, such as photographs, will have a mat sized to fit them. Cut all of the mats one inch larger than your piece of paper or photograph so that you have a border of mat showing around the edge.

These dimensions vary according to the size of your backboard and will not work with the smaller cardboard backboard.

Imagine your backboard for a minute. Do you prefer to write with a marker on a white background, or would you like to add a little color with a mat you can stick on the board? Draw a picture of what your backboard might look like.

Mat	Paper Size	Mat Size
Full mat	8½-x-11 inches	9½-x-12 inches
Half mat	8½-x-5½ inches	9½-x-6½ inches

Full Sheet	Half-sheet	Cut-to-Fit
Abstract	Purpose	Title
Procedure	Hypothesis	Photographs
Materials	Results	Drawings
Graphs	Conclusions	
Data tables	Some data tables	
Bibliography	Some graphs	
Research paper		

Mounting Mats and Papers

When you have marked the appropriate spaces on your backboard, prepare the mats. The easiest way to cut the mats is to use a large paper cutter. Be very careful. You may want to ask an adult to help you with this step.

Cut each mat to the size listed on the chart. If you want to mat your abstract, for example, hand-write or print a copy. Using a glue stick, put glue on the back of the paper and attach it to the mat. Be sure the paper is centered and wrinkle-free. Then, with double-sided tape, tape the mat to the backboard in the spot you've marked for the abstract. Prepare all of the single-sheet pages the same way and attach them to the board.

What Goes Where

Your teacher may suggest the layout of the board, or you can use these guidelines. Three items go on the left side of the board: the purpose, the hypothesis, and the abstract. First, measure from the bottom of the board going up, and with a pencil, mark a space for the abstract. It should be placed at least half an inch up from the bottom of the panel. However, don't stick anything on yet.

The remaining space on that panel can be divided in half for the purpose and the hypothesis. Measure and mark the space for those two items, giving them equal space. The purpose should be at least half an inch down from the top. Your first panel should look like this.

Now it's time to do the center panel. Make the space for the title of your project first. You may use vinyl stick-on letters to make the title stand out and attract the eye of the judge. Make sure the letters are not too bright or hard to read. For example, yellow letters on a white background are very hard to read. A dark mat behind the title makes it easier to read and looks attractive. Or you may print the title on paper. Make the letters larger than the type or printing you are using for the papers so that it can be easily read at a distance. Mount the title on a mat.

Place the title between half an inch and one inch down from the top of the board. Below the title you will need to make spaces for your data, any graphs, your materials list, the procedure,

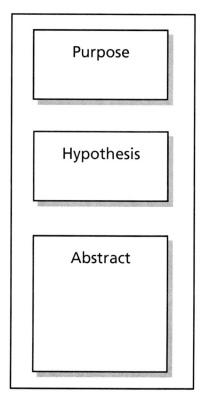

Left-hand panel of the backboard.

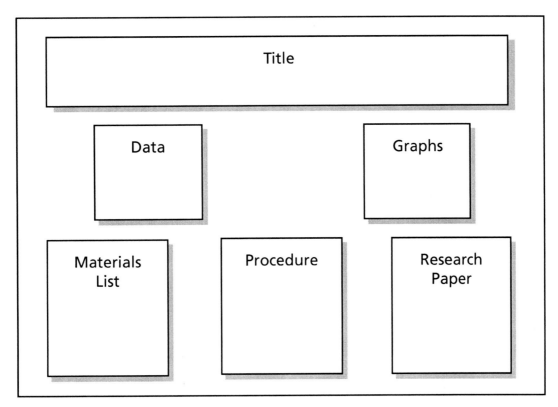

Center panel of the backboard.

and your research paper. Here's how the center panel might look. Yours may look a little different, depending on what elements you have.

Design the right-hand panel the same as the left side, marking spaces for the results, conclusions, and bibliography.

Titles

If you are using mats you don't need separate titles for each section. Just type the title (Purpose, Hypothesis, Abstract, etc.) on the paper above the text. Remember to use a larger font than the text so that it is easily read at a distance.

If you are not using mats, you may want to use special lettering for the titles of each section. Vinyl stick-on lettering looks nice, but can be expensive and you must have a very steady hand to put the letters on straight and even. If you do use them, be

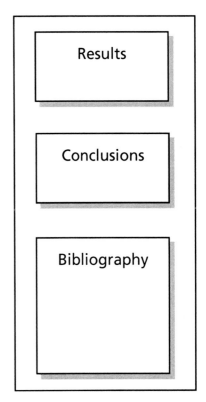

Right-hand panel of the backboard.

sure to draw a straight line with a pencil first as a guide, then carefully erase the line when you're done.

The letter "e" is the most frequently used letter. If you are using vinyl self-stick letters, be sure you have enough, all the same size and color. Use at least 2 in. high letters that can be easily read at a distance.

If you are using a cardboard backboard and marking pens, stick to two colors, one for titles and one for text. Dark colors on a light background are the easiest to read. Too many colors, bright or neon colors are distracting and difficult to read.

Get Creative!

This is your time to be creative. Let your backboard reflect your project and your personality. One student, doing a project testing lake water, drew a blue lake on her board and put the title of her project over it. Another student built an attractive backboard out of lattice-wood that looked like a fence panel for a project about backyard composting. Our sample project about milk might look good on a white backboard with black spots resembling a cow.

Don't overwhelm the viewer with too much detail or color, but make your backboard stand out and you'll be sure to attract the attention of the judges. Now let's get back to the other elements of the display and see how they work with the backboard to paint a complete picture of your project.

10 Make It Perfect

Finishing Touches

When your backboard is done, it's time to put the finishing touches on the rest of the display. The display includes everything you need to tell the story of your project. Think about including some of these other pieces as well:

- A table (and perhaps a tablecloth)
- Photographs
- Drawings
- Your research paper
- A reprints file
- Resource books
- Your logbook
- A computer
- A model

Write in your logbook what you will have as part of your display. Be sure to include anything extra that you might want to have on your backboard.

Table and Cloth

Science fairs are usually held in school classrooms, libraries, cafeterias, or gyms, and the school provides tables for students to use to set up their backboards. You may want to cover the table with a tablecloth. This is a nice touch that looks very professional. You can coordinate the color to match or complement your backboard, but be certain the cloth does not take up more space than your backboard is permitted. Since the only reason for the cloth is appearance, its use is entirely optional.

Photographs

Taking photos of your project every step of the way is an excellent way to show what you have done. Some of the photos can be mounted on the backboard, and the rest can be placed in an album as part of the display. Photos showing the results of the experiment are the most effective ones to place on the backboard. Pictures of the procedure should go in the album. If you include pictures of yourself performing some step of the experiment, be sure you are following correct procedure. For example, if in the photo you are handling chemicals, be sure you are wearing safety goggles.

Don't decorate the album or add anything more than a caption explaining what the picture is. When you take the pictures, think about what else is in the picture. You don't want a picture of your dog watching you perform the experiment. That's a great one for the family album, but not the science fair backboard!

It may be helpful to put a backdrop behind the experiment or model for the picture. A piece of matte (not shiny) black cardboard makes a good background. Be sure you have enough light to take a good picture. You may need to add a spotlight for additional lighting. A high-intensity desk light works well.

When you take a picture of the size of something, be sure to show how you made the measurement. A photo showing the height of plants, for example, should include your ruler.

Drawings

Can you tell the story of your project with drawings? If drawings or an illustration helped you design your project, include it on the backboard. You can also include a copy of the drawings with your research paper.

Here's a good idea: Whenever you display drawings or photographs, enclose them in a plastic sheet to protect them from fingerprints and smudges.

Research Paper

If you don't have a lot of tables, graphs, photos, or drawings on the center panel of your backboard, you can put a copy of your research paper there. The easiest way to do this is to mount it on a mat, as described in the previous chapter.

Whether or not you put a copy of your paper on the backboard, you need a copy for the judges to examine. This copy can be enclosed in a report cover, or you can consider putting each page in a plastic protector and using a three-ring binder to hold them all. This keeps the paper looking neat even after being handled by many people. You can put the bibliography at the end of the paper or in a separate binder if it is more than three pages long.

Reprints File

If you made photocopies of a number of magazine or newspaper articles for your background research, you can put them in a three-ring binder and add them to the display. This is called a **reprints file.** You may want to highlight the portions of the articles that you found helpful and that show the judges the specific information you used from that article.

Put a copy of your bibliography in the front of this binder to serve as a table of contents and organize the reprints in the same order as the bibliography.

Resource Books

If you have books that were especially helpful in your research, you can bring them to the science fair. Just stack them neatly on the table. Mark the pages where you found the most information with pieces of paper.

Logbook

Remember to bring the logbook you have been using every step of the way. It is a crucial part of the display. In fact, in some fairs you can be disqualified if it is missing!

The logbook is the scientific diary of your project. Everything you have done should be included, in the order in which you did it. The logbook is handwritten and never copied. Pages should not be torn from it. If you made a mistake in it, you should simply have crossed out that section and moved on to a new page.

Computers

Some students include a computer in their display. A computer program or video can illustrate what you have done. There are two cautions to using a computer in your display:

- Be sure the computer does not distract from your presentation. You must be able to present your project yourself. The computer should add to your presentation, but it cannot replace you.

- Be sure the computer is tamper-proof. If you cannot be present at your backboard throughout the entire fair, be sure the equipment is safe.

Technology is an effective way to display your project, but the personal touch is still always the best.

Models

Your project might be best displayed with a model. Or perhaps you used something during your experiment that can be displayed as a model. This is especially true of projects involving machinery or robots. If you experimented with airplane wing shapes, or tested aluminum baseball bats versus wooden bats, or studied different types of concrete bricks, then show them in your display. People enjoy seeing the actual objects you used in your project.

There are also some things you should *not* display. You may have used some of these things for your experiment, but you should not bring them to the fair:

- Live animals

- Plants

- Bacteria or viruses

- Mold

- Chemicals

- Food

Your teacher may also provide a list of things that cannot be displayed. It is very important to follow those rules. The student who performed the popcorn experiment had glued several popped kernels to her backboard. Luckily, her teacher noticed the popcorn before the science fair began and reminded her to remove them before a judge saw them.

The same guidelines apply to models that were given for computers. Models should not interfere with your presentation, and they cannot take the place of your presentation. If you have to leave the display, they should be tamper-proof. You may want to put a model in a see-through display case to protect it from inquisitive viewers who might otherwise try to touch it.

Effective Displays

Make your backboard and display come alive to tell the story of your project. Using our four sample projects, here are some suggestions for the backboards and displays:

"Will Milk Spoil Faster If It Is Left out of the Refrigerator?"

- Using a white background, draw large, irregular-shaped black spots. Mount your mats right over it so the background looks like a cow.
- On the center panel of the backboard, draw the inside of a refrigerator so that it looks like you have just opened the door of the refrigerator.
- Wash out a small milk carton and put it on the table in front of the backboard.

"Which Battery Lasts Longest?"

- Glue battery packages on the backboard.
- Display the flashlights you used in the experiment.

"How Does Acid Rain Affect Plants?"

- Use green as the color of your backboard or mats.
- Draw pots along the bottom of the backboard.
- Include photographs of the plants at different stages of their growth. (Be sure to show the ruler in the pictures.)
- Do not use live plants in the display. You can use empty seed packets to represent the plants.

"Does the Largest Popcorn Kernel Produce the Largest Piece of Popped Popcorn?"

- Use the popcorn's packaging to decorate the backboard.
- Use an empty popcorn box (the kind you get in a movie theater) in your display.
- Use yellow colors to remind the viewer of buttered popcorn.
- Include photographs of the popcorn and the ruler you used to measure the popped kernels.
- Draw a picture of an ear of corn on the background.

11 Give It Your All

The Science Fair

Wow! You've done a lot of hard work, and the day of the fair is right around the corner. It's time to think about this final part of your journey.

Have you ever presented a book report to your class? What you say and do at the science fair is a lot like giving a book report. You'll stand before a science fair judge or your teacher and talk about the highlights of your project. Unlike talking about a book report, this time you can give away the ending!

When you know that you have to stand up and speak before your class, how do you prepare?

- You choose your clothes carefully the night before.

- You practice what you're going to say.

- You write down a few notes for the important things you want to say so that you don't forget anything.

These are all great ways to prepare for any presentation, including the science fair. Some students feel nervous when they have to speak before their classmates or science fair judges. That's normal. Don't worry, though, this is really the easy part of the project! With all of the hard work you've already done, you're an expert on your project. Now you're just going to share what you've learned.

Dress to Impress

There is one last part of the display to think about—you! Most science fairs are not judged merely by looking at the backboard and checking the research paper. The judge wants to hear from you personally about what you've done and what you've learned from the experience. Just as you put a lot of effort into making your backboard look good, you want to make yourself look good for the fair too. The day of the science fair isn't just another school day. Dress nicely!

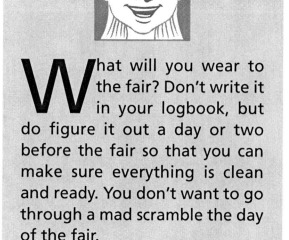

What will you wear to the fair? Don't write it in your logbook, but do figure it out a day or two before the fair so that you can make sure everything is clean and ready. You don't want to go through a mad scramble the day of the fair.

Wear what you might put on to go to a party or when your parents want you to dress up for a special occasion. Be sure your shirt is tucked in, your shoes are tied, and your hair is combed. And you'll want to wear comfortable shoes because you might have to do a lot of standing. Dressing up will make a good impression and help you to feel more confident.

Know What to Say

The best way to avoid feeling nervous at the fair is to practice your presentation ahead of time. Practice in front of a mirror, or your best friend, or your parents, or even your dog! Use your backboard to help you organize your thoughts. That's one reason why it is set up the way it is, so that you can refer to it as you talk about your project.

When someone walks up to your display, offer your right hand to shake his or her right hand and introduce yourself. Your first name is all that is necessary. Before you even begin, thank the person for their interest in your project: "Thank you for listening to my presentation."

Start by giving the title of your project. There are some things you will want to memorize, and this is one of them, but if you

Sample Opening Comments

- "The title of my project is 'Will Milk Spoil Faster If It Is Left out of the Refrigerator?' I was interested in this project because I always forget to put the milk away, and my mom tells me it will spoil if I don't."

- "The title of my project is 'Which Battery Lasts Longest?' I heard an advertisement that said Battery A would last longer than other batteries. I did this project because I like to go camping, and I wanted to know which battery lasts longest for a camping trip."

- "The title of my project is 'How Does Acid Rain Affect Plants?' I've read that acid rain can seriously damage crops in the United States. That could hurt farmers who grow the food we eat. I wanted to find out more about acid rain and how it affects plant growth."

- "The title of my project is 'Does the Largest Popcorn Kernel Produce the Largest Piece of Popped Popcorn?' I like to eat popcorn, and I wondered if there is a relationship between the size of the unpopped popcorn and popped popcorn."

get nervous and forget, remember that the information is right there on the backboard.

Next, explain why you wanted to do this project. (That's the "purpose," on the left side of the board.)

Now take a deep breath. The rest of the presentation is just as easy, so take your time. The judge wants to hear every word and then ask you a few questions. If the judge should interrupt you during the presentation to ask a question, just try to remember where you stopped. (You can look at your backboard to help you remember where to pick up again.)

The presentation is easy when your backboard follows the scientific method that you used in your project. The next part of the presentation is the hypothesis. Read it straight off the board and you can't go wrong! You've told the judge your title and why you wanted to do the project; now tell him what you expected would happen in the experiment.

Skip the abstract (next on the backboard). You can give the judge a copy if he doesn't already have one. Move on to the center panel of the board. Explain the procedure next. Here's the tricky part: You don't want to tell the procedure in as much detail as you wrote it for the paper and the backboard. But you do want to cover the most important steps. Think about that book report—you don't talk about every detail of the book. You simply include the important parts. Explaining your procedure is the same.

Stop! Don't go on to the results just yet. This is a good time to pause for any questions. Make sure the judge understands your procedure before you move on. You may point out any photos you

Sample Explanation of a Procedure

"I grew nine tomato plants from seed. Three were the control group, and I watered them with purified water. To simulate acid rain, I added vinegar to purified water. I labeled one solution 'Acidic.' It had a pH of 4.5. The other one I labeled 'Very Acidic'; it had a pH of 4.0. I watered three plants with the acidic water and three with the very acidic water. I measured the plants' growth after ten days and then every five days. I also checked their stems and leaves for any change in color or other effects."

took during the experiment. There's no need to go into detail about the materials list or the written procedure on the backboard. Skip the data table and graphs for the moment.

No questions from the judge? Then move to the right side of the backboard. You've displayed a paragraph about the results of the project without the tables and graphs. This is what you want to tell the judge, then you can show the data tables and graphs.

Sample Description of Results

"The plants that were given acidic water grew more slowly than the control group. The plants watered with acidic water had yellow and brown spots on their leaves. The plants that were given very acidic water grew the most slowly. Their leaves were very brown and shriveled. These plants actually died by Day 20."

What have you *not* said? You haven't explained about air pollution or plant pores or how you measured the pH of the water. All of this is background information that the judge may ask you about, but you don't need to talk about it if you're not asked. A simple explanation of your experiment, following the guidelines of the scientific method, is best.

After talking about the results, move on to the data tables and graphs.

Again, don't go into great detail. The purpose of the tables and graphs is to present the information at a glance. That is why you were so careful to choose the right type of graph to show your data. Let the judge look at your graphs, and if he has any questions, he can ask them.

Sample Description of Graphs

"As you can see from my graph, the control plants showed steady growth. The plants given acidic water also grew but were much smaller than the control plants. You can see that the plants given very acidic water also showed little growth.

"My photographs and tables clearly show the difference in the plants' leaves."

Sometimes you will have only data tables to show the judge. The data for the milk project, for instance, could not be illustrated with graphs.

Now you're ready for the conclusion of the project, and of your presentation. Go back to the right side of the backboard. Tell the judge your conclusion and whether it supported the hypothesis. That way you tie up the whole package neatly. It's okay if your experiment didn't support the hypothesis. You don't even have to explain why it didn't. The judge may ask why you think it didn't, or he may ask you whether you could have done something differently to get results that would have supported the hypothesis. Remember that it is okay if your experiment failed, as long as you followed the scientific method.

All Done?

Finish the presentation by showing the judge whatever you have on the table in front of the backboard. Let her take a look at your paper, your reprints file, your bibliography, your logbook, and any models. You don't have to say anything while she's looking. When she's all done, ask her if she has any questions for you. Lastly, thank the judge for looking at your project and listening to your presentation. Now, that wasn't so bad, was it?

What If the Judge Asks Me Something I Don't Know?

That is the number-one fear of science fair students. You won't know everything there is to know about your topic. The judge may know more about it. Remember that most adults think the science fair is a learning experience. You have learned a lot of new things just by doing the project. You can continue to learn the day of the fair.

BRAINSTORM!

Bring a fresh notebook with you to the science fair and write down any comments the judges make about your project, or any questions that you couldn't answer. These may form the basis of your next great project!

So if the judge brings up something you don't know, say so and tell the judge you'll look it up. The judge may even go ahead and tell you the answer. (If the judge does tell you the answer to his question, be sure to write it down and remember it! Another judge may ask you the same question.) Always be polite to the judges. They are there to help you learn from the whole experience.

What Do Judges Want to See?

Science fair judges are volunteers who are interested in science and in your experience with the science fair. They have a list of what they're supposed to look for in your project and presentation. If you understand what they want, you'll have a much easier time showing it to them.

Sample Judge's Checklist

- Student shows knowledge of the project by explaining it easily.

- Student shows use of the scientific method.

- Student shows enthusiasm and interest in the project.

- Student understands procedure and experiment.

- The backboard is well organized, clear, and visually appealing.

- The data tables and graphs are clear, easily understood, and appropriate.

- Student has written evidence of research, experimentation, and analysis of results.

You Be the Judge

You can help your student prepare for the science fair by listening as he practices his oral presentation. Pretend to be a judge. Say, "I'm your science fair judge; tell me about your project." Give your full attention. You can't be a science fair judge when you're reading the newspaper or making lunch. Don't interrupt to add parts of the story. Let him tell it all. When you do have suggestions, save them up until the end and phrase them as questions. "Do you think you might want to talk about how you watered all of the plants at the same time of day and with the same amount of water?"

Ask questions a judge might ask. Be sure your child has a thorough understanding of the scientific method and of the purpose of his project. Those are the two most important parts of a science project.

Encourage your student to practice the oral presentation as many times as necessary to become comfortable with speaking. Some kids are natural-born talkers; others need a little help. With practice, they can become comfortable with explaining the project (and they can fully understand what they've done).

12 You're a Winner!

The judging is over, and you have won! Perhaps you have a ribbon, a plaque, or a certificate to display. You're proud of all your hard work, and you should be! You took an idea, researched it, planned an experiment, did it, wrote a paper about it, and created a display. You explained the whole project to a judge and competed in a science fair.

Science Fair Skills

- Researching:
    - Selecting a topic
    - Learning how to find information in a library, in reference books, and on the Internet
    - Collecting and organizing information
- Experimenting:
    - Learning the scientific method and critical thinking
    - Developing the procedure for an experiment
    - Identifying tools, materials, and equipment for an experiment
    - Conducting an experiment
    - Identifying variables
- Dealing with data:
    - Keeping a logbook
    - Noting the results of an experiment
    - Analyzing data
    - Creating tables and/or graphs
    - Forming conclusions
- Writing a research paper:
    - Expanding spelling, grammar, and punctuation skills
    - Organizing information
- Presenting a project:
    - Designing and creating a backboard and display
    - Giving an oral presentation

Maybe you didn't win first, second, or third place. You did your best, but for whatever reason, you didn't win an award. You're still a winner! You started and finished a project, and you did it yourself. Be proud of your accomplishment whether you have a ribbon to show for it or not.

You've also mastered some new skills.

Whew! Did you realize that a science fair project could teach you that much?

What's Next?

If we told you that the answer to the question "What's next?" is "Next year's science fair," would you answer, "No way?"

You have done all the hard work of mastering new skills and learning how to do a project. Next year will be a lot easier. Your project may be one you want to continue working on, maybe by adding some new experiments and doing it again. Or perhaps you noticed someone else's project and are interested in researching something similar next year.

There are some excellent reasons to continue doing science fair projects. In junior and senior high school, the projects are much more complex and interesting and the awards even better. Students have received cash awards, scholarships, summer jobs, computers, books, and trips. Some students have even paid for their entire college education with scholarships won at science fairs.

When you participate in science fairs, you also gain self-confidence. You learn that you can take on a project and follow it through to completion. You grow in your ability to try new things, to work on your own, and to stick with it even when things go wrong. That doesn't mean you'll win first place every time, but you still learn valuable lessons, and if you keep on doing your best, you're a winner!

Beyond Your Local Science Fair

The fun and satisfaction you have found in learning new skills and exercising your problem-solving abilities do not have to end with finishing a science fair project. Many students who enjoy science research also want to participate in other related activities and competitions. Here are some of those other activities:

A Tale of Persistence

For years in elementary school, Heather struggled through mandatory science fair projects. While her best friend and her older siblings consistently won first-place ribbons at the fair, she often placed last. She mastered the scientific method and became comfortable with public speaking, but those things don't matter much to a fourth-grader. She wanted a blue ribbon to tack up on her bulletin board.

When she entered junior high school, her mother encouraged her to stick with science research. While her friends participated in orchestra, soccer, and drama, she was back in the lab, measuring agar for petri plates. But she was also learning persistence. Before long, scientific exploration became a reward in itself. In high school her hard work paid off in the form of awards, internships, college scholarships, even a two-week, all-expenses-paid trip to Europe.

In college she pursued other interests—she didn't become the next Marie Curie. But the lessons she learned from science fairs continue to have an impact on her adult work ethic.

Your children stand much to gain if they continue asking and investigating scientific questions and competing at science fairs. Don't nag or push—ultimately the decision must be theirs—but do encourage them to persevere in science research.

Other Competitions

- The Bayer/National Science Foundation Award for Community Innovation
- The Craftsman/National Science Teachers Association (NSTA) Young Inventors Awards Program
- Creative Competitions, Inc.'s Odyssey of the Mind
- The Discovery Young Scientist Challenge
- The Duracell/NSTA Invention Challenge
- FIRST (For Inspiration and Recognition of Science and Technology)
- Future Problem Solving
- The Intel Science Talent Search
- The Junior Science and Humanities Symposium
- The Science Olympiad
- The Toshiba/NSTA ExploraVision

Bayer/National Science Foundation Award for Community Innovation

Contact information:

National Science Foundation
4201 Wilson Boulevard
Arlington, VA 22230
Phone: 1–700–292–5111

Teams of four students, grades six through eight, work together to research a problem and develop an innovative solution in their own community. The deadline for project entry is the end of January, and prizes include an all-expenses paid trip to EPCOT, a $25,000 grant to develop the idea in the community, and savings bonds for each winning team member. Competition guidelines, tips for coaches, and entry forms are available at the National Science Foundation web site.

Craftsman/National Science Teachers Association Young Inventors Awards Program

www.nsta.org/programs/craftsman.asp

Contact information:

Craftsman/NSTA Young Inventors Awards Program
National Science Teachers Association
1840 Wilson Boulevard
Arlington VA 22201-3000
Phone: 1–888–494–4994
E-mail: younginventors@nsta.org

Do you enjoy designing and building your own inventions? Do you like to fix or improve things? In this program, students in grades two through five and grades six through eight compete by submitting a design for a unique invention. It might be a tool to fix something, to solve a problem, or to entertain. The students complete an entry form, keep a three to seven-page logbook, and submit a diagram of the tool and a photograph demonstrating the use of the tool.

The deadline is early March, and awards go to two national winners (one from each grade level), who receive a $10,000 U.S. savings bond, and ten national finalists (five from each grade level), who are each given a $5,000 U.S. savings bond. There are also $500 and $250 savings bond awards for third- and fourth-place regional winners. Every student who enters receives a certificate and a gift.

Creative Competitions, Inc.'s Odyssey of the Mind

www.odysseyofthemind.com

Contact information:

Odyssey of the Mind
c/o Creative Competitions, Inc.
1325 Route 130 South, Suite F
Gloucester City, NJ 08030
Phone: 1–856–456–7776
Fax: 1–856–456–7008
E-mail: cci@jersey.net

This is a creative problem-solving team competition that involves millions of students from around the world. Students from kindergarten through college compete in teams that tackle a problem in one of five categories: mechanical/vehicle, classics, performance, structure, and technical performance. Competitors are judged not only on their problem-solving but also on their style and teamwork.

Discovery Young Scientist Challenge

school.discovery.com/sciencefaircentral/dysc/index.html

Contact information:
DiscoverYoung Scientist Challenge
Science Service
1719 N Street, NW
Washington, DC 20036
E-mail: sciedu@sciserv.org

The Discovery Young Scientist Challenge is the only national science fair for students in grades five through eight. Directors of local fairs affiliated with the International Science and Engineering Fair nominate students, and the judges select four hundred semifinalists from these nominations, then forty finalists.

The finalists receive an all-expenses paid trip for a week in Washington, DC, where they compete in different scientific challenges and present their project before the other students and judges. The first-place winner receives a $10,000 scholarship, and all forty kids have the chance to appear on the Discovery Channel. Tell that to anyone who says that science research isn't glamorous!

Duracell/National Science Teachers Association Invention Challenge

Contact information:

Duracell/NSTA Invention Challenge
National Science Teachers Association
1840 Wilson Boulevard
Arlington VA 22201–3000
Phone: 1–888–494–4994

This national competition is open to students in grades six through twelve, working alone or with a partner. They design and build a device that runs on batteries, write a two-page description of the device and its practical uses, draw a diagram, and send a photograph with the entry form. The deadline is early January. Winners receive savings bonds, and their teachers receive gifts.

FIRST

www.usfirst.org

Contact information:

200 Bedford Street
Manchester, NH 03101

Phone: 1–800–871–8326
Fax: 1–603–666–3907
E-mail: info@usfirst.org

FIRST, which stands for "For Inspiration and Recognition of Science and Technology," sponsors two annual competitions. Students ages nine through fourteen can participate on one of the 1,500 teams in the FIRST LEGO League. With an adult coach, usually an engineer, teams tackle a scientific or technological problem and use LEGOS to construct a robotic solution to it. The FIRST LEGO League also holds a weeklong summer science camp and a robotic competition for high school students. Participants can win a trip to EPCOT for national competition and college scholarships.

Future Problem Solving

www.fpsp.org

Contact information:

Future Problem Solving Program
2028 Regency Road
Lexington, KY 40503
Phone: 1–800–256–1499
E-mail: FPSolve@aol.com

The Future Problem Solving (FPS) Program challenges students in grades four through twelve to consider societal issues and creatively design solutions to these problems. There are several components to FPS, including team problem-solving, action-based problem-solving, individual competition, community problem-solving, and scenario writing. The problems are very applicable to everyday life and encourage students to explore the complex issues in their own communities and in the world.

Intel Science Talent Search

www.sciserv.org/sts

Contact information:

Intel Science Talent Search
Science Service
1719 N Street, NW
Washington, DC 20036
E-mail: sciedu@sciserv.org

This intensive and prestigious competition is open to students in secondary school, so it's something to consider for the future. Students submit their original research report as well as essays, letters of recommendation, and school records. From those submissions, three hundred semifinalists are selected and awarded a $1,000 scholarship. Forty finalists are chosen from that group and travel to Washington, DC, to compete in the final competition.

Over $530,000 in scholarships are awarded to these finalists, with the first-prize winner taking home a $100,000 scholarship. These students are in good company—five alumni of the talent search have won the Nobel Prize, and ten have been awarded MacArthur Foundation "genius" grants.

Junior Science and Humanities Symposium

www.jshs.org

Contact information:

JSHS
24 Warren Street
Concord, NH 03301
Phone: 1–603–228–4520
FAX: 1–603–228–4730
E-mail: cousens@jshs.org
E-mail: trojano@jshs.org

Also for slightly older students, the Junior Science and Humanities Symposium is sponsored by the U.S. Army, Navy, and Air Force in cooperation with leading research universities throughout the nation. Over ten thousand high school students attend forty-eight regional symposia and present their original research before peers and the academic community. The first-place winner at each regional competition is awarded a $4,000 undergraduate scholarship and receives an invitation to present his or her research at the national symposium.

Science Olympiad

www.geocities.com/soincus

Contact information:

Science Olympiad
5955 Little Pine Lane
Rochester, MI 48306

Phone: 1–248–651–4013
Fax: 1–248–651–7835
E-mail: Soinc@soinc.org

Students involved in the Science Olympiad compete in teams and as individuals in disciplines that include biology, earth science, chemistry, physics, and computers and technology. Don't let the heavy topics deter you—the competition is a blast! Open to students in grades kindergarten through twelve, it is modeled after popular games, TV shows, and sporting events. Last year over 13,500 elementary and secondary teams from Canada and all fifty U.S. states participated in Science Olympiad programs. Check with your school to join or start a team.

Toshiba/NSTA ExploraVision

Contact information:

Toshiba/NSTA ExploraVision
National Science Teachers Association
1840 Wilson Boulevard
Arlington VA 22201–3000
Phone: 1–888–494–4994

This is another competition open to all students, grades kindergarten through twelve, in the United States and Canada. Students work in teams of two, three, or four with a team coach and an optional mentor. Each team explores some aspect of technology relevant to their lives. Then they explore what that technology might be like twenty years in the future. They must communicate their ideas through a written description and five graphics-simulating web pages. The entry deadline is early April.

Twenty regional winners receive a laptop computer for their school. First- and second-place teams receive savings bonds of $10,000 and $5,000 and take a trip to Washington, DC (with their parents) for the award ceremony. Other prizes include Toshiba digital cameras. Every student who participates receives a certificate and gift. Coaches and mentors also receive prizes.

Glossary

abstract A one-page summary of your science fair project; limited in length to a maximum of 250 words.

average The sum of all the samples divided by the number of samples.

backboard The display of your science fair project; generally consists of three attached panels.

background General researched information concerning your topic of study or experimental question.

bibliography A list of source materials or references compiled during research of your topic, generally appearing at the end of your research paper.

citation A quotation from source material, with credit to the source given in parentheses, a footnote, or an endnote.

conclusions A statement explaining why the experiment results either proved or rejected the hypothesis.

control The experimental group that is not changed in order to serve as a standard of comparison during experimentation.

data The information or results of experimentation, often expressed in the form of numbers or statistics.

format The way a research paper is set up.

graph A diagram or visual representation of your data.

hypothesis   The prediction of the results of your experiment.

ISEF   The International Science and Engineering Fair, held annually for grades six through twelve.

key words   Words or terms for the significant concepts and facts from a project idea that aid in research because they can be looked up in library card or computer files or on the Internet.

logbook   Your detailed, chronological record of your research and experimentation.

materials list   A list of the materials and equipment needed to carry out an experiment.

null hypothesis   A negative expression or the opposite of the prediction of the results of your experiment.

plagiarism   The representation of someone else's work as your own; copying another person's work.

procedure   A step-by-step plan or recipe describing how to perform your experiment.

purpose   A statement of the practical application of your project.

qualitative observations   Subjective observations of experiment results that cannot be measured in numbers and instead are described in words.

quantitative observations   Objective observations of experiment results that can be measured and expressed in numbers.

reprints file   A three-ring binder with photocopies of the source materials used in background research, for display with a science fair project.

results   The answer to the question posed by a project hypothesis.

run   An experimental trial.

scientific method   The set of problem-solving steps used by scientists.

source   The place where information is found during research, such as a magazine article, an Internet web site, or an encyclopedia entry.

trial   In experiments, a test; also known as a **run.**

variable   The experimental group that is changed and compared to the control.

Index

abstract:
  backboard layout, 80, 82–84
  in presentation, 98
  writing tips, 72–73
acid rain, sample project:
  abstract, 73
  effective display for, 92
  experimentation procedure, 36, 68
  hypothesis, 30–32, 66
  information gathering, 19, 21, 25
  line graph, 58
  materials list, 68
  observations, 46
  purpose, 66
  research paper, 66–68, 70
  results, 58
  sample index card, 25
  tables, 48–49
affect/effect, use of, 70
air pollution, information gathering, sample index card, 25
alphabetical order, in bibliography, 69
analysis skills, 104

animal projects:
  for Grades 4–6, 12
  for Grades 1–3, 11
  hypotheses, samples, 31–32
  information resources, 23
  working with animals, tips for, 39
attitude, importance of, 3
audiotapes, of observations, 51
averages, in results, 55–56, 62
awards, 3, 105–106

backboard:
  building/construction guidelines, 78–80
  cardboard, 77–78
  color, use of, 81, 83–84, 86, 92–93
  creativity with, 86
  defined, 77
  elements of, 81
  judge's checklist for, 101
  layout, see Layout, backboards
  lettering tips, 78, 84–86
  mats, 81–84
  multiple pages, 81
  presentation, use in, 98

  problems with, 80
  size of, 77–78
  tables on, 54
  titles, 84–86
  transporting, 77, 80
  types of, 77
  where to buy, 78
  working with, tips for, 78
background information:
  in abstract, 72
  in research paper, 67
background research, 30. See also information gathering
bacteria, information resources, 23
bar graphs, 56–57
batteries, sample project:
  bar graph, 57
  effective display for, 92
  experimentation procedures, 35, 38–39
  hypothesis, 31–32
  information gathering, 19
  materials list, 41
  results, 55–57
  topic selection, 19
  tables, 47, 55–56

Bayer/National Science Foundation Award for Community Innovation, The, 107
bibliography:
    in abstract, 73
    backboard layout, 82, 85
    reprints file, 90
    in research paper, 67, 69
binders, in display:
    reprints file, 90
    research paper, 89
biological projects:
    defined, 4
    for Grades 4–6, 12–13
    for Grades 1–3, 11–12
    ideas for, 11–13
    information resources, 23
    sample, 19
birds:
    color preferences, 31–32, 38
    food preferences, 11
book citation, sample, 27
brain, information resources, 23
brainstorm! tips:
    data organization, 56, 61
    display planning, 76–77, 83
    experimentation, 34, 38–40, 42
    hypothesis, 30
    materials list, 40
    information gathering, 18, 21
    presentation, 96, 100
    record-keeping, 50
    research paper, 72
    topic selection, 4, 6, 8

cardboard backboard, see backboard
cause-and-effect relationships, 3, 30–31
chemicals, working with, 39, 89
Chicago Manual of Style, The, 74

citations:
    importance of, see plagiarism
    in information gathering, 26–28
    in research paper, 65
color:
    on backboard, 81, 83–84, 86, 92–93
    in bar graphs, 57
    in line graphs, 57
    in pie charts, 60
competitions, see Related activities/competitions
computers:
    diagram/graphing programs, 57, 62
    in display, 88, 90–91
    information gathering, 26. See also Internet
    information resources on, 23
    labels, for backboard mats, 82
    projects involving, 15
    spell-check, 70
    spreadsheets, 62
    word-processing programs, 66
conclusions:
    in abstract, 73
    backboard layout, 81–82, 85
    defined, 2
    in presentation, 100
    in research paper, 69–70
controls, in experimentation:
    observations, 47–48
    types of, 36–39
Craftsman/National Science Teachers Association (NSTA) Young Inventors Awards Program, The, 107, 108
Creative Competitions, Inc.'s Odyssey of the Mind, 107–108
creativity, 3, 104
critical thinking, 104

data:
    analysis skills, 104
    backboard layout, 84–85
    dealing with, 104
    organization tips, 24–26, 53–62
diagrams:
    graphs, see graphs
    pie charts, 59–61
    use of, 42
Discovery Young Scientist Challenge, The, 107, 109
displays, see Backboard
    computers, 88, 90–91
    drawings, 88–89
    effective, 76, 92–93
    ineffective, 76
    logbook, 88, 90
    materials needed for, 82
    models, 88, 91
    photographs, 88–89
    planning tips, 76
    in presentation, 100
    research paper, 88–89
    reprints file, 88, 90
    resource books, 88, 90
    table and cloth, 88
    tamper-proof, 91
    what not to include, 91
    what to include, 88
disqualification, reason for, 77
documentation, see Record-keeping
    index cards, 24
    logbook, 6, 8, 18, 21, 24, 48, 49, 56
drawings:
    in display, 88–89, 93
    use of, generally, 42
dress code, 96–97
Duracell/NSTA Invention Challenge, The, 107, 109

editing, research paper, 70
effect, use of, 70
electricity, safety tips, 39

encyclopedia:
    citation, sample, 28
    as information resource, 24
endnotes, 65
enthusiasm, importance of, 3
environmental projects:
    defined, 4
    for Grades 4–6, 15–16, 19
    for Grades 1–3, 15, 18
    ideas for, 15–16
    information resources, 23
    sample, 18–19
experimentation:
    controls, 36–39
    defined, 2, 5
    materials, 39–40
    problems, dealing with, 42
    procedures, 34–35, 41–42
    safety precautions, 39, 43
    skills development, 104
    variables, 36–39, 43
expert interview, citation,
    sample, 28
experts:
    contact information, 24
    as information resource, 23,
    28
eye safety, 89

FIRST (For Inspiration and
    Recognition of Science and
    Technology), 107, 109–110
foam-core display board, *see*
    backboard
footnotes, 65
format, of research paper, 66
future problem solving, 107,
    110

graphs, *see* Pie charts
    bar, 56–57
    backboard layout, 80, 82,
    84–85
    importance of, 61
    labeling, 57–59
    line, 57–59

in presentation, 99, 101
    purpose of, 54
    in research paper, 72
    title for, 57
Greenhouse effect, 16

handshake tips, 97
health topics, information
    resources, 23
horizontal axis, in bar graph,
    57
hypothesis:
    in abstract, 72
    backboard layout, 80, 82–84
    defined, 2, 30
    null, 32
    in presentation, 98
    proof/support of, 32, 52, 69,
    100
    rejection of, 32
    in research paper, 66, 69
    sample, 31

illustrations, 42. *See*
    also diagrams; graphs
independent projects, benefits
    of, 5, 7
index cards, information
    gathering:
    citations, 27, 69
    information organization,
    24–26
information gathering, *see* data
    citations, of information
    sources, 26–28
    current resources, 24
    defined, 2
    highlighting, 26
    importance of, 18
    information resources, 20, 23
    Internet, 20–21, 24
    key words, 20–21, 23
    organizing information,
    24–26
    types of, 24
    where to look, 20, 23

Intel Science Talent Search,
    The, 107, 110–111
International Science and
    Engineering Fair, 109
internet:
    citation, sample, 27
    in information gathering,
    20–21, 24

judge(s):
    comments from, 100–101
    disqualification by, 77
    questions from, 98–99,
    100–101
    research paper for, 89
    respect for, 101
    sample checklist for, 101
Junior Science and Humanities
    Symposium, The, 107, 111

key words, in information
    gathering, 20–21, 23

labeling:
    bar graph, 57
    line graph, 58–59
    pie charts, 60
laboratory safety, 39, 43
layout, backboards:
    center panel, 80–81, 85, 92,
    98
    graphs, 80
    left-hand panel, 80, 84
    using mats, 81–84
    multiple pages, 81
    planning, 78
    right-hand panel, 81, 85, 99
    tables, 80
    titles, 82, 84–86
    what goes where, 84–85
lettering tips, for backboard,
    78, 84–86
librarian, help from, 21
library, information gathering,
    20
line graphs, 57–59

logbook:
  in display, 88, 90
  display planning in, 76
  experimentation procedures,
    34, 38, 42
  hypothesis, 30
  information gathering, 18, 21
  key words, 21
  materials list, 40
  purpose of, 6
  qualitative observations,
    48–51
  tables in, 56
  topic selection, 8
logical reasoning, development
  of, 3

magazine(s):
  citation, sample, 27
  as information resource, 24
  in reprints file, 90
materials list:
  backboard layout, 81–85
  elements in, 39–40
  in research paper, 67–68, 72
mats, on backboard:
mounting tips, 83–84
  use of, 81–83
measurements:
  assistance with, 52
  daily, 46, 50
  photographs of, 89
  recording, 47–50
  types of, 46, 50
metric measurements, 46
milk, sample project:
  effective display, 92
  information gathering, 18, 21
  materials list, 40
  procedures, 35
model(s):
  building, 23
  in display, 88, 91
*Modern Language Association
  Handbook for Writers
  of Research Papers, The,* 74

National Science Foundation,
  contact information, 107
National Science Teachers
  Association, contact
  information, 107–108, 112
newspaper articles, in reprints
  file, 90
nitrogen, in plants, 11
null hypothesis, 32

observations:
  graphs, *see* bar graphs; line
    graphs
  measurements, types of, 46
  qualitative, 46
  quantitative, 46
  in pie charts, 59–60
  records of, *see* record-keeping
Odyssey of the Mind, contact
  information, 107
opening comments, in
  presentation, 97
oral presentation:
  answering questions, 98–101
  appearance, 96–97
  backboard, use of, 98
  of display materials, 100
  judges checklist, 101
  opening comments, 97–98
  practice for, 96–97, 102
  preparation for, 96
  purpose, statement of, 98
  questions from the judge,
    98–101
organization tips:
  index cards, in information
    gathering, 24–26, 69
  for results, 53–61
  tables, for observation
    results, 47
outline, for research paper, 64

parenthetical citations, 65
parents:
  attitude, impact of, 3
  backboard building tips, 79

help from, 24, 42, 62
information gathering,
  assistance with, 24
Internet guidelines, 22
involvement of, 7
materials, providing, 40
presentation review, 102
project ideas, 10
research paper review, 71, 74
safety review, 39, 43
support from, 3, 52, 106
people, projects about:
  for grades 4–6, 12–12
  for grades 1–3, 11
percentages, in pie charts,
  59–60, 62
persistence, importance of, 106
personal appearance, 96–97
Photographs:
  backboard layout, 82–83, 92
  in display, 88–89, 92
  in presentation, 98–99
  qualitative observations, 51
physical projects:
  defined, 4
  for grades 4–6, 14–15
  for grades 1–3, 13–14, 19
  ideas for, 13–15
  information resources, 23
  sample, 19
plagiarism, 22, 65–66
plant project, sample:
  abstract, 73
  effective display for, 92
  hypothesis, 30–31
  information gathering, 21,
    23, 26
  information resources, 23
  key words, 21
  line graph, 58
  materials list, 41, 68
  procedures, 68
  research paper, 66–68
  results, 58
  sample index card, 26
  tables, 48–49

plant projects:
  for grades 4–6, 12, 15–16
  for grades 1–3, 11, 15
  sample, *see* plant project, sample
  variable groups for, 37
pollution, information resources, 23
popcorn, sample project:
  effective display for, 93
  experimentation procedure, 37–39
  hypothesis, 31
  information gathering, 19, 21
  materials list, 41
  observations, 46, 50
  topic selection, 15, 37, 39
potatoes, electricity generation, 14
practice tips, for oral presentation, 97–100, 102
"practical application," 6, 8
preparation tips:
  daily measurement, 46, 50
  for oral presentation, 96
  time management, 5, 34
  topic selection, 2, 4
presentation, *see* oral presentation
presentation skills, 104
prizes, 105
problems, dealing with, 42
problem-solving, 3, 8
procedure, in experimentation:
  in abstract, 73
  application of, 41–42
  backboard layout, 81–85
  photographs of, 88–89
  in presentation, 98
  in research paper, 67–68, 72
  sample, 34–35
project ideas, generally:
  biological projects, 11–13, 19
  environmental projects, 15–16, 19
  physical projects, 13–15, 19

proofreading, 70
purpose:
  backboard layout, 80, 82–84
  defined, 6, 8
  in presentation, 98
  in research paper, 66

qualitative observations, 46–47, 50
qualitative results, showing, 54. See also Diagrams; Graphs
quantitative observations, 46–47, 50
questions:
  for information gathering, samples, 21
  in presentation, 98, 100–101
  in topic selection, 2, 4–5

record-keeping:
  importance of, 42, 46
  tables, 47–50
  tips for, 50
reference books, 74
related activities/competitions:
Bayer/National Science Foundation Award for Community Innovation, The, 107
Craftsman/National Science Teachers Association (NSTA) Young Inventors Awards Program, The, 107, 108
  Creative Competitions, Inc.'s Odyssey of the Mind, 107–108
  Discovery Young Scientist Challenge, The, 107, 109
  Duracell/NSTA Invention Challenge, The, 107, 109
  FIRST (For Inspiration and Recognition of Science and Technology), 107, 109–110
  Future Problem Solving, 107, 110

  Intel Science Talent Search, The, 107, 110–111
  Junior Science and Humanities Symposium, The, 107, 111
  Science Olympiad, The, 107, 111–112
  Toshiba/NSTA ExploraVision, The, 107, 112
report cover, 66, 89
reprints file, in display, 88, 90
research paper:
  backboard layout, 81, 85
  background, 67
  basic outline, 64
  bibliography, 67, 69
  computer-typed, 66
  conclusions, 69–70
  in display, 88–89
  editing, 70
  format, 66
  handwritten, 66
  hypothesis, 66
  length of, 72
  materials list, 67–68, 72
  photographs in, 89
  procedure, 67–68, 72
  proofreading, 70
  purpose, 66
  report cover, 66
  results, 68–69, 72
  rough draft, 66
  title, 66
  writing skills development, 104
research skills, 104
resource books, in display, 88, 90
results:
  in abstract, 73
  averages, 55–56
  backboard layout, 81–82, 85
  diagrams/graphs, 54, 56–61
  photographs of, 88
  in presentation, 99
  qualitative, 54

results (continued)
    quantitative, 54
    in research paper, 68–69, 72
    runs, number of, 54–56
    trials, number of, 54–55
rough drafts, of research paper, 66
runs, defined, 54

safety:
    in experimentation, 39, 89
    importance of, 5
sample projects:
    acid rain 19, 35, 41, 46, 92
    batteries, 19, 35, 38, 41, 92
    milk,18, 21, 35, 40, 92
    plants, 19, 35, 41, 92
    popcorn, 19, 37–38, 41, 46, 92
scale:
    in bar graph, 57
    in line graph, 58–59
scholarships, 3, 105
school laboratory:
    assistance in, 43
    working in, 39
science fairs competitions, generally:
    awards/prizes, 105
    lessons learned from, 104, 106
    related activities/competitions, 105, 107–112
    skills development, 104
Science Olympiad, The, 107, 111–112
scientific method:
    applications, generally, 32
    defined, 2
    importance of, 42, 69, 101
    understanding of, 101–102
self-confidence, development of, 105
speaking skills, 3, 104. See also oral presentation

spelling, checking tips, 70–71
success factors, generally, 3

table and tablecloth, in display, 88
tables:
    backboard layout, 80
    in presentation, 99–101
    purpose of, 47, 54
    in research paper, 69
    tips for, 47–50, 54
teacher:
    backboard layout tips, 84
    display guidelines, 80, 91
    help/advice from, 23–24, 39–40
    topic approval from, 6
temperature, in record-keeping, 46
test group(s):
    defined, 36
    multiple, 55–56
thank-you notes, 24
time management, 5, 34
title(s):
    backboard layout, 82, 84–86
    for graphs, 57–59
    for pie charts, 60
    in presentation, 97
    in research paper, 66
    for tables, 47
tools to use, see backboard; displays
    circular protractor, 60
    computers, 57, 62
    crayons/markers, 57, 59, 62
    ruler, 59
to/two/too, use of, 70
topic approval, 6
topic selection, see specific subjects
    biological projects, 4, 11–13, 19

environmental projects, 4, 15–16
importance of, 2, 7
independent projects, 5, 7
physical science projects, 4, 13–15, 19
safety concerns, 5
suggestions, 7
teacher's approval, 6
Toshiba/NSTA ExploraVision, The, 107, 112
trials, defined, 54
types of projects:
    biological, 4, 11–13, 19
    environmental, 4, 15–16, 19
    physical, 4, 13–15, 19

up-to-date information, importance of, 24

variables, in experimentation:
    defined, 36
    importance of, 37, 43
    sample, 38
vertical axis, in bar graph, 57
videotapes, of observations, 51
vitamins, information resources, 23

"who cares" factor, 6, 8
winning, 104
Woe is I (O'Connor), 74
wood backboard, construction tips, 78–80
word-processing programs, 66
writing tips:
    abstracts, 72–73
    reference books, 74
    research papers, 3, 64–72

yellow Pages, information resource, 23

LaVergne, TN USA
01 February 2011
214701LV00001B/3/P